Benni & Victoria

Friends Through Time

by
Patricia H. Aust

illustrated by Robert Sprouse

Child & Family Press ❦ Washington, DC

This book is dedicated to my husband, Erich,
for helping me become reasonably computer literate
and building me an office I could call my own,
and to my father, Charles H. Hinckley (1913–1993),
who always knew I'd publish.

❦

The present-day scenes from *Benni & Victoria* are set at "Oak Grove School," an institution whose main building and unused chapel architecturally resemble the main building and chapel at Oak Grove-Coburn School in Maine, my son Jay's wonderful preparatory school that closed in 1989. The interior and overall condition of the "Oak Grove" chapel and the 1858 "original" school building, however, are figments of my imagination, as are all the characters. Any resemblance of the characters in *Benni & Victoria* to Oak Grove-Coburn staff or students, either living or dead, is unintended and purely coincidental.

It should also be noted that "Oak Grove School" is not meant to be the portrayal of an ideal, average, or substandard institution. Rather, it is a fictional compilation of the many programs for children receiving out-of-home care that I've worked in, observed, read about, heard about, or been interested in throughout my career.

My grateful thanks go to Eileen Hehl, Linda Harmon, and Laura Aust for their ongoing support and excellent suggestions in the fine-tuning of this manuscript, and to all Connecticut Chapter RWA members, whose friendship, similar struggles, and warm encouragement kept me going.

Child & Family Press is an imprint of the Child Welfare League of America

© 1996 by Patricia H. Aust. All rights reserved. Neither this book nor any part may be reproduced or transmitted in any form or by any means, electronic or mechanical, including photocopying, microfilming, and recording, or by any information storage and retrieval system, without permission in writing from the publisher. For information on this or other CWLA publications, contact the CWLA Publications Department at the address below.

CHILD WELFARE LEAGUE OF AMERICA, INC.
440 First Street, NW, Suite 310, Washington, DC 20001-2085

CURRENT PRINTING (last digit)
10 9 8 7 6 5 4 3 2 1

Cover illustration by Robert Sprouse; cover design by Jennifer Geanakos
Text design by Eve Malakoff-Klein
Printed in the United States of America
ISBN # 0–87868–629–0

Library of Congress Cataloging-in-Publication Data
Aust, Patricia H., 1942-
Benni & Victoria : friends through time / by Patricia H. Aust :
illustrated by Robert Sprouse.
    p.   cm.
Summary: In residential placement as a result of his mother's substance abuse ten-year-old Benni travels back in time to befriend a nine-year-old girl during a diphtheria epidemic.
ISBN 0–87868–629–0
[1. Time travel--Fiction.   2. Drug abuse--Fiction.   3. Puerto Ricans--United States--Fiction.   4. Diphtheria--Fiction.   5. Foster home care--Fiction.]   I. Sprouse, Robert, ill.   II. Title.
PZ7.A91986Be   1996
[Fic]--dc20   96-25674

April 1995

Sunday night, Benni was so hungry, even water didn't stop the ache in his stomach. Where was Mommi?

He opened the refrigerator and ate the last of the mustard, but his stomach still hurt. He looked in the wall cabinet again. All he could see on the top shelf was the edge of a couple old plates.

He dragged a chair over to the counter and climbed up. Maybe there was something on the top shelf. He stood on his tiptoes and looked. Nothing but dust.

Sadly, he wiped his hands on his filthy jeans. How could he go to school like this?

Maybe he should call the hospital. His heart beat faster, remembering two weeks ago when he couldn't wake Mommi up after school. He'd run downstairs for Alma, and she'd called 911. What if no one was with Mommi this time? Maybe she was dead!

Suddenly, someone pounded on the door. Benni jumped off the chair and rushed to open it. Mommi must have forgotten her key!

It was Mr. Gonzalez, their landlord. He lived downstairs and he knew all about Mommi. Pushing past Benni, he looked around the messy apartment.

1

"Where's your mother? The rent was due Friday."

"She'll be back later."

Mr. Gonzalez opened the refrigerator. When he saw it was empty, he checked the cabinets over the sink.

Benni watched, his hands in his pockets. Mr. Gonzalez better not tell the State about this. They'd take him away this time for sure.

Mr. Gonzalez looked sad. "You hungry?"

Benni nodded. "A little. Could I have some rice?"

An hour later, he felt better. He'd drunk a glass of milk and eaten the big bowl of beans and rice Mrs. Gonzalez had given him. He'd also used up the last of Mommi's soap, but his hands and face and shirt were clean enough for school now.

"Benni, let me in!"

This time, a young white man stood next to Mr. Gonzalez. "Benni Ramirez, meet Jakob Howard, a social worker from the State. He wants to talk to you."

Benni's muscles turned to jelly. *The State put parents in jail. They put kids in foster homes.*

He was so stupid. The first time Mr. Gonzalez came upstairs, he should have hidden under the bed. If he hadn't answered the door, Mr. Gonzalez would have gone away. He wouldn't have seen the empty refrigerator or Benni's dirty clothes.

Benni sank into a kitchen chair and hoped he would say the right thing so Mommi wouldn't get in trouble.

December 1995

Chapter 1

Benni shivered the first time he saw Oak Grove School. It didn't belong on this country road. It didn't fit in with the ordinary houses and trailers, the rundown farms. It had suddenly appeared as they rounded the last curve: a huge, brown building from another time, looming darkly from the top of a snow-covered hill.

Ivy crept up its brick walls toward a fortress-like roof. Heavy vaulted doors anchored it to barren meadows.

Benni was sure it was haunted.

Jakob, his social worker, nodded toward the place. "That's Oak Grove School, your new home."

"It doesn't look like a school," Benni said. "And I'm not staying here. I told you, Mommi's taking me home today."

"I know that's what you want, Benni, but remember, she's just coming to visit. Whatever happens, I think you'll like Oak Grove. It's a nice place."

"That's what you said about my foster homes, too, all three of them."

Jakob sighed. "I know you've had bad luck, especially with Mrs. Perez. She liked you a lot."

"Right."

Jakob's long fingers smoothed his tightly curled black hair and short, bushy beard. "She did like you, Benni, but she needed your bedroom for the new baby."

Benni shrugged. "Whatever." He pulled his jacket sleeves over his bony wrists and wished his jeans were a little longer. He was still skinny, but he'd grown a lot taller since he turned ten. He wondered if Mommi would notice.

The edges of Oak Grove's driveway were piled with snow, more snow than the city had seen so far. Jakob pointed to a small church on their left as they drove toward the main building. "See that? Used to be Oak Grove's chapel."

Big deal.

They parked in front of a grove of winter-bare oak trees with more meadows behind them. Benni didn't like so much open space. He liked his own neighborhood: dark alleys, apartments, boarded-up houses, cars and people everywhere.

Where do you hide around here?

Jakob turned off the engine. "Ready to meet Mr. Bolton?" he asked.

Benni opened his door. "No, ready to see my mother."

They walked around the car and Jakob unlocked the trunk.

"I'll take your clothes," Jakob said, picking up two paper bags.

Benni grabbed a small cardboard box. It held the few things he'd brought from home: a picture of Mommi, a card from Uncle Luis, a Field Day award, a small Puerto Rican flag.

Jakob closed the trunk. "Okay, let's go."

Benni's heart thumped. He hadn't seen Mommi since last spring when she'd shown up at his first foster home and taken him out for ice cream. "I'm getting a job," she'd said. "I'll bring you home by Three Kings Day—January sixth—at the latest."

Her curly brown hair had hung limply over swollen, tired eyes and she was so thin it scared him.

A few days ago, she'd called again and promised to visit him to-day, December 28.

She'll be here, I know it.

The school looked even bigger and gloomier up close. Jakob paused at the tall double doors in the center of the school, his hand on the doorknob. "Any questions before we go in?"

"No," Benni said. He didn't need to know anything. He wasn't staying here.

They stepped into a large entry hall. In front of them, a wide stairway curved up and to the right, ending in a balcony that doubled back over their heads. The wide, rubber-treaded stairs were dark and battered; the walls a dingy white.

Jakob dropped Benni's bags on a narrow table near the front door. Benni slid his treasure box behind them and took off his jacket.

"Wait here while I find Mr. Bolton, okay?" Jakob's steps echoed on the bare wooden floor as he disappeared around a corner. Somewhere down the hall, a clock ticked and dishes rattled.

Benni felt edgy. It was too quiet. If this was a school, where were all the kids?

Nervously, he pushed his brown hair off his forehead and looked around. Game room and library to the left, offices to the right, and beyond those, a large dining room and kitchen.

Click, STOMP. Click, STOMP. Benni jumped at the sound of heavy footsteps on the balcony overhead. Someone was moving toward the stairs. His heart pounded again.

Where was Jakob?

He noticed an open office door. Maybe he could hide in there until Jakob came back. Tears stung his eyes. No, probably not allowed. That was the problem with moving. He didn't know the rules.

When he heard someone on the stairs. Benni ran to a small door under them, opened it, and found a low closet with metal chairs stacked to one side. Quickly, he entered and shut the door, crouching so he wouldn't hit his head.

The closet was so dark, he couldn't see his hand, yet he saw a small cloud of grey-white smoke at the back. It had no heat or smell and it shimmered with faded colors. Curious, he reached out to wave it away, then jumped when it darted to and fro and shot through the ceiling like a wingless bird.

What was that?

Breathing deeply, he tried to slow his racing heart. Maybe his *premonicion*, that first, frightened feeling when he saw Oak Grove, was right. Maybe this place was haunted.

The heavy footsteps passed the closet and faded away.

Benni pressed his ear against the cold door, wondering whether he should stay where he was or look for Jakob.

"BENNI! HEY, BENNI! Where are you?"

Was that Jakob, or was it a trick?

"BENNI! Come on, it's Jakob."

Jakob.

Benni pushed on the door handle and fell into the hall. He blinked his eyes in the sudden light.

Next to Jakob stood a tall, thin man dressed in a suit and tie. He didn't look old, although his hair and mustache were grey.

"Ray, this is Benito Ramirez," Jakob said. "And Benni, this is Mr. Ray Bolton, director of Oak Grove."

Mr. Bolton smiled and shook Benni's hand. "Sorry we kept you waiting for so long."

Benni pushed his hair off his forehead again. "Where's my mother?"

Jakob frowned. "I'm sorry, Ben. She's not here. We tried to reach her just now, but couldn't. It looks like she's moved."

Benni's heart skipped. *Where was she?*

They'd lived in that apartment for six years. Why would she move? She liked it there.

He grabbed Jakob's arm. "You sure you told her the right day? Did you write to her in time?"

"Yes," said Jakob.

Benni was scared. Something was really wrong. Mommi must have run out of money. She must be sick or in a hospital. He started for the front door. He wasn't staying in this stupid place. He was going back to his old neighborhood. They'd know where she was. He'd live in cellars if he had to, but he'd find her. He'd tell her he was sorry for getting her in trouble.

Jakob grabbed him and held him tightly. "Benni! Hold on! I know how much you want to see your mother. We just tried calling her, but her phone's disconnected. We talked to your landlord, too, but he doesn't know where she is."

"But you said she'd be here!"

Jakob relaxed his hold on Benni's arm. "No, I said I'd tell her when you were moving, and I did. That's why she called you. I'm sorry, Ben. Come on, let's go to Mr. Bolton's office and talk."

Benni wiped his eyes and followed Jakob and Mr. Bolton down the hall. Served him right. He never should have asked Mr. Gonzalez for rice in the first place and he should have told Jakob Mommi was at the store.

He was a bad son, talking about his mother. From now on, he wasn't telling grown-ups anything. If he didn't talk to them, he couldn't get Mommi in trouble, and maybe she'd come back.

Before they reached Mr. Bolton's office, Benni's rage and fear had turned to stone. He could handle this, no matter what they did to him. He shrugged Jakob's hand off his shoulder. He didn't need pity. He was getting what he deserved.

Mr. Bolton's office was large and crammed with beautiful old furniture. Benni slumped into a chair and watched a strip of light poke through the drapes and slide across the rich red rug. It cast flickering shadows on his shoes and made him sleepy.

He watched it until Jakob and Mr. Bolton stopped asking questions and left him alone. Until they knew he had shut them out.

It was easy.

Chapter 2

Benni's room was on third floor. Up there, the walls were light green and the carpeting tan, but the woodwork was dark brown, like everywhere else.

"Most of the boys up here are your age," Mr. Bolton said as he unlocked a door at the end of the hall. "One's older, but he's moving to a group home soon."

Benni's stomach clenched. A group home—another fake family where grown-ups were paid to take care of kids.

"Of course," Mr. Bolton said, "We'd rather see our kids go home when they leave, or get adopted."

Benni's throat tightened. He wasn't getting adopted. Mommi could take care of him, once she found a job. He was older now, anyway. He could take care of himself.

Mr. Bolton stepped back so Benni and Jakob could enter the small, narrow room ahead of him. Benni dropped his box on the bottom bunk and emptied a bag of socks and shirts near it.

Mr. Bolton nodded at the tall dresser and grey lockers opposite the bunk beds. "You get the two bottom drawers, Benni, and the left locker. Looks like your roommate has the bottom bunk, judging from the way it's made."

Benni threw his socks into the third drawer.

"Your roommate's David Pukowski," Mr. Bolton continued, "But everyone calls him Pookie. He's a good kid. I'm sure you'll get along. So, finish unpacking, then join us for lunch."

Jakob rubbed his flat stomach and smiled. "Thought you'd never ask, Ray." He upended the other bag and started putting jeans and underwear in the bottom drawer.

Benni looked around. The bunk bed was pulled out from the wall just far enough so he could tuck in the blanket without scraping his fingers. Next to it, in front of the only window, was an old wooden chair.

This place is too neat, Benni thought, and the carpet too clean, not like a real home. He flopped onto the chair. He was sick of moving and tired of everything.

Jakob sat on the edge of the bed. "I know this is hard, Benni. You've moved three times this year already. At least you won't have to leave Oak Grove if someone gets pregnant or sick."

How about if I hit kids when they steal my stuff or make fun of my mother?

Jakob folded up the paper bags and put them in the waste basket. "Ready for lunch? The food's pretty good here."

Benni almost answered, then remembered. *Keep your mouth shut if you want to see Mommi again.* He twisted around and looked out the window.

"What's with the silent treatment?" Jakob asked. "I can't help you if you won't tell me how you feel."

Why should I? It never helped before. I still had to move. I still couldn't live with my mother.

Jakob sighed. "Never mind. Let's go to lunch, okay?"

Benni's stomach started to growl as they hurried downstairs. He'd been too nervous to eat breakfast and he could smell hamburgers.

Jakob grinned. "Our favorite lunch, right?"

Benni stood at the dining room door and stared. Light brown, long wooden tables with benches on both sides filled the room. Massive wooden beams crossed the high, peaked ceiling and a stone fireplace covered half of one wall.

Benni liked the cloth banners that hung from the beams, the student pictures, the holiday decorations. He liked the noise. The room was full of kids, mostly boys.

At a wide counter that separated the kitchen from the dining hall, Jakob handed him a plastic tray. "Help yourself."

Benni took a hamburger, chips, an apple, and three cookies from the big metal bowls on the counter, then waited while Jakob filled glasses with milk from a dispenser on the wall. Jakob looked around. "These guys look okay," he said, choosing a table near the kitchen, where a young man and woman were talking.

"Hi, social worker," the young woman said, as Jakob and Benni sat down. She was tall, black, and pretty, with long wavy hair.

"Hi, Seronda," Jakob said.

"Are you Benito Ramirez?" she asked Benni.

Benni nodded, sat down, and took a big bite out of his hamburger. It wasn't juicy in the middle like Mrs. Perez's, but it tasted pretty good.

"Well, it's nice to meet you." Seronda said, smiling. "I'm your new teacher, Ms. Williams." She motioned with her head toward the man sitting next to her. "This is Seth Tyler, another teacher."

"Hope you play basketball," Seth said. "Seronda's class could really use some help."

Too bad. I'm outta here, first chance I get.

Benni stuffed a cookie into his mouth and gulped his milk. Maybe they'd leave him alone if he kept his mouth full.

Ms. Williams looked at Benni, waiting for a reply.

Jakob shrugged his shoulders. "Benni's been kind of quiet today, Seronda."

She nodded. "Going to a new place is hard. Once Benni settles in, he'll be as noisy as the other kids."

"Probably," Jakob agreed, drowning his hamburger in ketchup and mustard. "When do afternoon classes start?"

"After recess usually, but today we have teacher training, so the kids will do something fun with their dorm counselors instead."

"Hey, lucky you," Jakob said.

Benni looked away as tears stung his eyes.

Yeah, lucky me. Lucky, lucky me.

Chapter 3

Twenty minutes later, Jakob had left and Benni huddled behind the school with the other fourth, fifth, and sixth grade boys. Although the group was somewhat protected by the gym wing on one side and the library wing on the other, the blustery wind whipped across the meadow and found them anyway.

Benni glanced up at his window, looked away, then looked back. Had he seen someone there? He blinked. Yes, someone small stood behind the panes. He wondered who it could be, since all the kids were outside.

Suddenly, Ronnie, their live-in counselor, and Tito, a classroom aide, each raised an arm.

"Listen up!" Ronnie barked. He was tall and black, with short hair. He definitely pumped iron.

Another blast of icy wind slapped at their heads.

"Where are your gloves?" Ronnie asked two boys. They shrugged. Ronnie sighed. "Who else needs gloves?" Two hands went up.

"Okay. Pookie and Whip, go find eight mittens or gloves in Lost and Found. You have five minutes."

Pookie? Benni stared at the tall, chunky blonde boy with the big smile as he raced the other kid to the back door.

Great, his roommate was white as the stupid snow. Why didn't they give him a Puerto Rican roommate, someone who'd understand why he had to be home for Three Kings Day? Not some honkie who didn't even know what Three Kings Day was.

Ronnie smiled. "Guess we're ready for our scavenger hunt."

Suddenly, Ronnie motioned to Benni. "Come here, Ben."

"Guys, this is Pookie's new roommate, Benni Ramirez. He's in fifth grade, and I hear he's fast with the basketball." He smiled down at Benni, his long fingers resting on Benni's shoulders. "Is that right, ma man? You good on the court?"

Benni shrugged.

A black boy near Benni said, "Hey, welcome Ben. I'm Dwane. I'm the team manager."

Benni looked him over. Manager? Dwane had to be the smallest, skinniest manager on earth.

Ronnie had the boys separate into two groups and picked team captains. "Okay, here's a list of things your teams have to find and a laundry bag." He looked at his watch. "It's two o'clock. That gives you forty-five minutes to find your stuff. Everything you need is outside. Remember, no one goes inside without permission and STAY WITH YOUR BUDDIES!"

Benni listened while Whip, captain of his group, explained how the scavenger hunt worked. "Okay losers, listen up. You find somethin', ya give it to me and I cross it off the list. If our team finds everything first, we get extra goodies on Saturday night. Got it? Now count by fours to find your buddy."

Dwane whooped when he realized that he and Benni were buddies. Benni ignored him. He was wondering if he should talk to kids since he wasn't talking to adults. He decided he'd have to, since he'd be with them day and night. Besides, the kids had nothing to do with bringing Mommi back.

The wind suddenly started up again, piercing Benni's jacket and biting at his wrists. His toes ached from the cold and he couldn't stop shivering.

Whip held up the team's list. "HEY, IS EVERYBODY LISTENIN'?"

The kids stopped talking.

"Okay, here's what you gotta find. Twelve acorns, a bird's nest, a pink stone, two different pieces of paper, something yellow, something soft, and something from summer. Easy, except for the bird's nest."

"I'LL FIND IT!" Dwane yelled.

Whip looked over at Ronnie and Tito who were pacing up and down the driveway, their hands in their pockets. "Dwane, don't forget what Ronnie said. You and your *buddy* will find the bird's nest, right?"

"HERE'S MY BUDDY!" Dwane yelled, grabbing Benni's arm.

"Big whoop," Whip sneered. "Now, get goin' and bring back the loot."

Benni looked at Dwane's friendly, shining face. He didn't care who his buddy was, as long as they got moving and warmed up.

A few minutes later, Benni cared. Dwane kept stepping on his heels and he talked nonstop.

"Ben, where we gonna find the nest? Behind the school? How 'bout the field over there? How old you are? I'm nine. Where you from? I'm from somewhere far, I don't remember. You ever go to New York? I'm in fourth grade, 'spose to be in fifth. What grade you in? Where you play basketball before?"

Benni scowled and said nothing.

He and Dwane looked in every tree near the school building and behind the garage, but didn't find any nests near the ground. Then Benni remembered the trees around the chapel. If he got rid of Dwane, maybe he could find a nest there, break into the chapel, and warm up.

He put his arm on Dwane's shoulder. "Hey, buddy, see those bushes behind the school? Bet there's a nest there. Let's split up and meet at the garage in twenty minutes."

"YEAH! LET'S GO!" Dwane yelled.

Benni watched Dwane hop away. *Good thing he forgets rules fast.* He wondered what happened if you got caught without your "buddy."

As soon as Ronnie and Tito were busy with other kids, Benni

dashed across the driveway, and made it to the chapel without getting caught. He found a small, tattered nest on the ground behind
the chapel. Smiling, he stuffed the nest under his jacket.

Time to get warm.

Benni groaned when he found the back door of the chapel locked.

Great. What next?

He tried to pull boards off a small window in the foundation, but
they wouldn't budge, even when he wedged a piece of lumber behind them. At least he was warmer now, working so hard.

He walked back to a narrow door on the side wall and lifted its
metal latch, but the door was locked from the inside. Leaning hard
against it, he pushed and pulled until something inside loosened
and the door gave. He stepped into a narrow passageway and hurried down the worn stone steps at the end of it.

Benni stood on the bottom stair and looked around. He was in
the cellar of the chapel. It was so dimly lit that he could barely make
out the old tables and chairs scattered about.

He jumped as he heard a shrill whistle and hoped it didn't mean
the scavenger hunt was over.

Crossing the landing, he ran up another flight of stairs, opened
the door at the top, and burst into a dim, dusty foyer. To his right
were double doors that led outside. He opened a pair of narrow
doors on the left and found himself in the main part of the chapel.

The only light in the room came from the edges of the boards on
the tall side windows. A shredded piece of red cloth hung from one
of them. Wires dangled from a hole in the ceiling.

A few dark wooden pews faced a bare altar and more were stacked
at the back of the room near the choir loft stairs. Hesitantly, he
stepped further into the room.

This place wasn't like his church. Not even close.

"ANYBODY HERE?" he yelled, then slapped his head.

Smart, Ramirez. What if someone outside heard you?

BUMP, bump, bump!

What was that?

He ran under the choir loft and hid behind a stack of pews. The
noise had come from overhead. Maybe there was an animal up there,
or a street person. He wasn't waiting around to find out.

Benni jumped up, forgetting to steady the pews in front of him. One fell on his frozen foot and the others thumped heavily to the floor.

"OW, OW, OW!" he yelled, grabbing his sneaker and hopping around on one leg. When his leg started aching too, he sat down, his eyes clenched shut, and rubbed his throbbing toes.

Whoever was in here knew exactly where he was, but his foot hurt too much for him to stand up. He rested his head on his knees and waited for the pain to subside.

For a couple minutes, he heard nothing. Maybe there was no one here after all.

Tap, tap... Tap, tap.

What was that?

He listened again, barely breathing. He wasn't alone.

"Who is downstairs?" a voice called.

Benni's breath came out in a rush. There was nothing to fear. This was a squeaky little voice, a girl's voice! But what was a girl doing in the chapel?

He opened his eyes, then shut them as blinding sunlight made them tear. He blinked, opened them again, and felt his heart skip in his chest. Trembling, he stood up and turned in place.

The afternoon sun streamed through clear, shiny windows that were hung with heavy red drapes. Matching cloths decorated the altar and a gleaming pulpit. The walls and high ceiling were snowy white and thick evergreen boughs decorated the choir loft.

Halfway down the chapel's center aisle, an iron, woodburning stove warmed the room. High overhead hung a polished brass light. Carved straight-back chairs stood on the altar and shiny brass candlesticks adorned the table.

"Why did you cry out, boy? Did you hurt yourself?"

That little voice again!

Benni whirled around and looked up at the choir loft. Leaning over the banister was a tiny, pretty little girl. Her serious face was surrounded by red pipe curls caught up in a large, fluffy bow on top of her head. Her eyes were large and so intensely blue they reminded Benni of the sea around Puerto Rico.

He rubbed his eyes. He must have knocked himself out when the

pews fell and this was a dream. Where had the ugly old chapel gone and who was this girl? He hadn't seen any girls this small at Oak Grove, or any redheads, either.

Benni tried to smile, but his face felt frozen.

Slowly, he climbed the choir loft stairs, his eyes locked on hers. She watched him, her face reflecting his own amazement and fear as her eyes moved downward from his ragged haircut to his brown face and hands, his old jacket, and his worn-out sneakers.

He could see she wasn't poor like him. He could tell from her clothes. Polished buttoned boots shone on her feet and thick white stockings covered her legs. Her green plaid dress was covered with a frilly white apron and ruffled, lacy pants peeked from below her long, puffy skirt.

She was beautiful and precious, like a doll he'd seen in a museum one time, but she wasn't real.

"Who are you?" she asked in a chirpy little voice.

Benni tried to speak, but nothing came out. He stepped into the choir loft and looked around. A small organ stood near the banister. On each side of it were shining pews and in the corner, a heavy, hooded cape lay on a chair.

"A cape," he said in wonder. "An old-fashioned coat!"

His heart raced. The cape. Heat from a stove. Polished, beautiful wood. This was Oak Grove chapel, but he was in an earlier time!

Suddenly, Benni's legs trembled as if he'd run for miles. How did he get here? How would he get back? How would Mommi and Jakob know what had happened to him if he stayed here?

He stood still as the little girl looked at him. She had freckles on her pale cheeks and confusion in her beautiful blue eyes. Maybe she was afraid, too.

What can I say that won't scare her even more? What can I tell her when I don't understand this myself?

The girl solved the problem by speaking first. "I am Victoria Morgan," she said, her voice quivering a little. "And you are a specter, are you not?"

Chapter 4

Benni stared at her. "A specter? What's that?" He didn't like the way she raised her chin and looked at him like he was stupid.

"Why, a specter," she said, "is a spirit, of course, a ghost. Are you not a ghost?"

"NO, I'M NOT A GHOST, TINKERBELL!" Benni yelled. "I'm a kid! Are YOU a ghost?"

Victoria sniffed. "Of course not. You cannot see my hand through the railing, can you?"

Benni looked down and shrieked. His hand wasn't brown any more. It wasn't even solid. It was a pale, almost colorless cloud that went through the railing when he moved it.

He looked at his other hand. Same thing. Grabbed his face, but couldn't feel it. Saw polished wood planks through his shoes.

"WHAT'S HAPPENED TO ME?" Benni cried. "I'm a ghost!" Tears rolled down his cheeks. "I'm dead."

Now he'd never find Mommi or go home to the red brick buildings of his neighborhood, the wide, noisy sidewalks and crowded storefronts. Where were they now?

Victoria walked toward him. "I do not think you are dead. I am not dead when I come to your time," she said.

Benni's mouth dropped. What was she talking about, coming to his time? Was she a ghost, too? How could she be so calm about it?

He was getting out of here. The instant he thought of leaving, he dropped, weightless, to the bottom of the stairs. He wondered if he could fly, and found himself high above the chapel, whooshing from altar to choir loft, from floor to ceiling, just by thinking about it. He flew through the wall behind the choir loft, dropped to the foyer, then zipped up to the loft again.

It was amazing, but it wasn't fun.

He stopped in front of her. "Victoria, I can fly! How? And how do I get back to my own time? Mommi and Jakob will worry about me. I'm worried about me. Look, I'm not real any more."

He grabbed at a sheet of music on the organ, but couldn't hold it. He tried to kick the organ bench, but his leg waved like a curtain in the breeze. He couldn't even walk without floating.

Tears he couldn't feel ran down his cheeks. "I'm not big, but I'm strong, Victoria. At least I was." He looked at his strange, see-through hand again. "Now I'm a cloud! I'm nothing!"

He hovered near the railing, not knowing what to do or where to go.

Victoria held up her hands. "Please, boy, try to be calm. Tell me your name, and where you come from."

Benni wiped his eyes. "I'm Benni Ramirez, from Portland, Maine. When I woke up this morning, it was December 28, 1995."

Victoria's eyes widened. "I have visited other times, but have never talked to anyone from 1995. And Ra-mir-ez, 'tis an unusual name."

"I'm Puerto Rican."

"Puerto Rican?"

"Puerto Rico's an island south of the United States. I was born there, and came to America when I was three. I live at Oak Grove School now."

She looked surprised. "It is called Oak Grove School in 1995? We call it Oak Grove Female Seminary. We do not have boys here. Do your parents work in the kitchen?"

Rage choked him. She could tell he was poor from his old clothes

and was rubbing it in. "NO, MY PARENTS DON'T WORK IN THE KITCHEN!" he shouted. "DO YOURS?"

Victoria jumped, but her strong little chin jutted forward again. "No, they do not. I am sorry if I offended you. My aunt is Mrs. Mary Tyler, founder of Oak Grove Female Seminary, and she teaches here. My mother sent me here from our house in town so I would not catch diphtheria from my little brother, Edward."

"How old is he?"

"Four years."

"How old are you?"

"Nine years, last week."

He stared at her tiny body, her little feet. She was almost as old as he was, but she looked six at the most.

"Why don't you stay with your father somewhere else?" Benni asked curiously.

Tears sprang to Victoria's eyes. "My father is in Europe on business for another month. Mamma said I must stay with my aunt until Edward has recovered and they are sure that no one else in the household has diphtheria. 'Tis very easy for children to catch it, you know."

Benni shook his head. "No, I never heard of it. What's dif-ther-ia?"

Victoria sighed. "It is a cruel disease. Children often cannot move or breathe after they catch it. Sometimes they sicken and die in but two or three days."

She sat down on a pew near him, her little hands clasped tightly in her lap. "My cousin Nell died of diphtheria last month, and seven of our neighbors' children died this week, as well. I do not wish to get sick, but I do want to go home. I miss Mamma and Edward so much."

A strange disease and old-fashioned, fancy clothes. Wanting to know, but afraid of the answer, Benni asked, "What is the date today?"

"Why, 'tis December 28, eighteen hundred and fifty-eight," Victoria said with a smile.

The same day, but 1858!

Then he remembered. "You said you've visited other times besides this one. How?"

Victoria shrugged. "I am not sure how I get to other times. It sometimes happens when I hear a loud noise in the Seminary buildings, like I heard you cry and yell just now. Then I try very hard to see what is happening, and find myself in a different time."

"But you're not a ghost now," Benni said.

"No, because you came to my time. You are a ghost in my time; I am a ghost in your time. That is what happens. I do not know why, but that is what happens."

Benni's head spun. He was a ghost in her time, because he didn't exist in 1858. That's why the chapel looked so beautiful and clean. It was new! Somehow, he'd ended up at Oak Grove in 1858, when it was a private girls' school.

Victoria smiled shyly. "I am glad I found you, because I need your help. I must know if Edward is getting better."

Benni flew to her side. "Why doesn't your mother tell you how he is? Why doesn't she call you, or write?"

"Call me? Town is three miles away. How could I hear her call me?" Victoria looked confused.

"I mean, on the telephone."

"The tel-e-phone?"

Benni thought for a minute. Maybe telephones hadn't been invented yet. "Do you have a telegraph office?"

"Not nearby," Victoria said sadly.

"The mail!" Benni said.

"The mail stage comes but once in a week and my mother is too busy caring for Edward to write to me. My aunt does not dare go to our house these days, for fear of bringing diphtheria back to Oak Grove with her."

Benni sighed. "Then how can I help you? I'm..." He looked at his wispy body. "I'm nothing."

"You could go to town and find out how Edward is. I am not allowed to leave."

Benni looked at Victoria's sad, pinched little face. She needed her mother, too, and she needed to know if her little brother was all right. Maybe he could help her, even if his body felt useless. She seemed like a strong little girl, asking a stranger for help. Maybe she'd tried this before.

"Have you talked to anybody else from another time?" he asked.

Victoria nodded. "Yes, I did, many years ago, before they closed the chapel, before your time."

"What happened?"

"Nothing," she said angrily, "I met a girl and she agreed to take the turnpike to town, but as soon as I left the chapel, I left her time." She wiped away a tear. "I never saw her again."

"How did that girl find you, Victoria? Did she yell and knock over pews like me?"

Victoria smiled. "No, I heard her singing my favorite hymn, 'Abide with Me,' as she was dusting the organ." Her eyes took on a dreamy look. "The chapel was very beautiful that day. That smelly stove was gone, and a lovely red carpet ran down the center aisle."

In a clear, sweet voice, she began to sing "Abide with Me." Benni didn't understand all the words, but her singing made him feel calm.

When she finished, he clapped his filmy hands silently. Victoria giggled and curtsied. "Thank you, sir. I am grateful you found me this time, instead of that lazy girl. You are much more fun."

"But how did I find you? I wasn't singing."

"I am not sure. I usually hear music better than noise, but I did hear someone yell, and I heard you crying."

"I heard a big bump in the choir loft before you came. I thought an animal or a homeless person was up here."

Victoria giggled. "Sarah knocked over the organ bench when she left to get some music for me. Perhaps you heard that. You must have a special gift, Benni. I don't think everyone can hear me."

"I'm not special," Benni muttered.

Except that I'm talking to a girl from 1858 like it was nothing.

He closed his eyes and concentrated on today and yesterday. He remembered everything. He knew what was real. He definitely wasn't crazy. Feeling better, he opened his eyes.

Victoria was still there.

"Listen," he said. "It's tough you can't go home and find out how Edward is, but at least you have a home and you know where your family is. You've got to help me get back to my own time. I have nowhere else to go and no idea where my parents are."

Victoria's mouth dropped. "You do not know where your parents are?"

He wondered why he was telling a ghost his private business, but he had to tell somebody. He couldn't tell adults any more, and Dwane or Pookie would blab for sure. But who could Victoria tell if he was the only one who'd seen her?

At least he wasn't cold anymore. Cold! He jumped and looked toward the windows. The scavenger hunt must be over! He had to go back, fast. Dwane must be looking for him. Ronnie must be looking for him! He spun around.

"Victoria, maybe I can help you, but not today. I have to go back to my own time, fast. How do I do that? You must know! You've gone to other times."

"Yes, I have." She looked at the floor. "But if I leave the chapel, my time will leave with me. Then you shall be gone, and..."

"PLEASE, GO!" Benni shouted. "I'LL TRY TO FIND YOU AGAIN. I'LL COME BACK AND CALL YOU, I PROMISE!"

"Very well." Sadly, Victoria put on her cape and started down the stairs. "I hope you speak the truth," she said, "and will return. I need your help."

Benni sighed. He didn't like being a ghost and he wasn't sure he could help her, but he knew how it felt to have no news of your family and to worry about them day after day.

"I'll try to find you again," he said softly, "And I'll try to find out about Edward, I promise. Just leave. I've been gone too long. I'll be in trouble!"

"Good-bye, Benni."

He watched as Victoria ran out the front door.

Instantly, the choir loft smelled only of dust. It was dim again, and cold.

Benni felt his way down the stairs, his hands gripping the banister. He was back, back from talking to a girl who was long dead. He must have imagined the whole thing.

No. He'd just felt the chapel turn cold and seen bright sunlight flicker out like a candle. The floor felt gritty under his feet again, instead of shiny and new.

Already, he missed his tiny little friend.

Sadly, he stepped into the biting wind, years and years away from Victoria's beautiful chapel and the warm yellow light.

Chapter 5

It wasn't quite New Year's Eve, so the dining hall still looked like Christmas. A big tree sparkled in the corner, and paper chains decorated the windows and walls.

To Benni, everything looked the same as the day he came to Oak Grove, but everything was different, because of Victoria. The world seemed bigger and older; time moved backward and forward. Victoria existed somewhere.

Impatiently, he pushed thoughts of Victoria out of his mind. She might still be around, but he wasn't sure he'd have time to help her. Maybe he wouldn't even be able to find her again.

After supper, he stirred his ice cream, wondering how fast he could get out of this stupid place. If he followed all the rules and didn't fight, Mr. Bolton would tell Mommi how great he was doing. Maybe she'd be so proud of him, she'd stop drinking and doing drugs, and Jakob would let him go home.

Ronnie raised his hand as the boys finished their dessert. "Okay, Table Two, listen up. I wanna hear everybody's New Year Resolutions."

Suddenly, Benni's ice cream didn't look so good. "Here's where I get in trouble," he told Pookie.

"Why?" Pookie asked, pushing his straight blonde hair off his forehead.

"You know I don't talk to adults, only kids."

Pookie shrugged. "No problem. I'll talk for you. Mom says I've got the gift of gab."

"Thanks," Benni said. He needed somebody on his side.

"HEY, RONNIE!" Dwane yelled. "I GOT A REVOLUTION!"

Benni cringed at Dwane's mistake when he saw Stew's mouth curl into a sneer. Stew was thirteen, tall, wiry, and mean, especially to the little kids.

"Rev-o-lution?" Stew mocked, looking cross-eyed at Dwane. "Duh. Did you say rev-o-lution?" He raked his wide, flat fingers through his greasy brown hair and trained his ratty little eyes on Dwane.

Dwane jumped up and leaned into Stew's face. "YOU LAUGHIN' AT ME, FOOL?"

Dwane swung at Stew, but Benni caught his arm and Dwane punched the bench instead. "JERK!" he yelled.

Ronnie stood up. "That's enough, you two! Are we gonna fight, or are we gonna say what we resolve to do better next year?" He pointed at Stew. "You—quiet! Okay Dwane, what's your resolution?"

"I'm gonna do my work and get all A's and B's."

"Right, Braindead," Stew muttered.

"Go for it, Dwane!" Pookie said, his chubby face widened with a smile.

"How 'bout you, Pukowski?" Ronnie asked.

"I'm gonna make two goals every game in spring soccer!"

"YES!" one of his teammates yelled.

Benni wished he could turn invisible as Ronnie went around the table. He had a New Year's resolution. In fact, he had two: "Don't talk to adults," and "Be good so you can go home." He just wasn't telling anybody, that was all.

Ronnie stared at him. "Benni, what's your resolution?"

Benni stared at his ice cream soup. *Suck an egg, Ronnie, I'm not talking.*

Stew clasped his hands as if in prayer. "Oh, please, Benni, pa-lease tell us your resolution. We're just dyin' ta hear it, honey buns!"

Benni felt his temper roll into a tight fist in his stomach. *Say one more thing, scumbag, one more thing...*

Pookie jumped up. "I know Benni's New Year resolution, Ron! He wants to be Student of the Month, twice, like at his last school."

Thanks, Pook. Now everyone will think I'm Mr. Nerd.

Stew made little kissing noises. "Oh, how nice. And you know exactly how to do that, don't ya, sweetie?"

The fist in Benni's stomach exploded. No one called him a brown-noser, especially a jerk like Stew!

He shot off the bench, grabbing his milk and ice cream. He threw the milk in Stew's face, put his ice cream bowl on the floor, and pulled Stew to the floor.

Stew was so surprised, he flipped onto his hands and knees. Right away, he tried to stand up, but Benni sat on him and poured ice cream down his back.

"WAY TO GO!" Pookie yelled.

Benni grinned. *Thank you, buddy. Oops.*

Ronnie yanked Benni off Stew and pulled him away from the table. "Calm down, Benni, you hear?"

Keep your shirt on, Muscles. I'm fine now.

Benni knew he shouldn't have jumped Stew, now that he was thinking clearer, but it sure felt good to see Stew squirming around while Whip tried to wipe the cold stuff off Stew's pants and shirt with a fistful of napkins.

Benni smiled until he realized that the kids in the dining hall weren't watching Stew any more. They were staring at him and Ronnie.

Uh, oh.

"Listen up, Benni," Ronnie said sternly. "You need to learn this real fast if you want to stay out of trouble. Insults are part of living here. Get used to it. If someone's mean, that's their problem. If you hit 'em for it, that's your problem, and your time-out. Now let's go."

Benni followed Ronnie to the time-out room near the kitchen, his head down so he couldn't see anybody laughing at him.

"I'll tell you when your time's up," Ronnie said.

The door shut with a soft thud and the light went on. Benni looked around. No windows, no rug, no nothing. Jail.

"It's not locked," Ronnie said from the other side of the door. "Just be quiet and think about what I said."

Benni leaned against the wall, then slid to the floor. He didn't feel so good any more.

It didn't matter if Stew started the fight, or if Stew was a bully. Stew wasn't in the closet. He was out there laughing at him.

Benni wondered what happened to his resolution to follow the rules so he could go home.

If he didn't watch his temper from now on, he'd be here forever, like Victoria.

Chapter 6

On Parents' Night, Benni sat down behind Pookie and Mrs. Pukowski near the back of the gym. Metal chairs had been set up in rows to face a small stage at the front of the room. The basketball hoops had been folded away and the large, echoey room was softly lit. Adults and children were still moving around. They talked and called to each other, adding to the confusion.

Benni could hardly sit still as Mr. Bolton walked to the center of the stage, but not for the same reason as most of the other kids. Some of them were nervous because they'd soon be performing in the talent show; others were excited because their relatives were already there.

Benni felt like a windup toy. Every muscle in his body was ready to spring toward the door when Mommi arrived. He knew she'd come. Tonight was January 5th, the eve of Three Kings Day, his and Mommi's favorite holiday.

He remembered when he was little, in Puerto Rico, how Mommi always told him the story of the three wise men on January 5th. Before he went to sleep, they'd slide a box full of straw under his bed for the wise men's camels. As he slept, Mommi and Poppi would go from house to house with their friends, singing, dancing, and eating special dishes.

The next morning, Three King's Day, Benni would find the camels' box full of little presents and the straw gone.

Benni jumped when Pookie shook his arm. "Earth to Ramirez! Is your mother comin'?"

Benni nodded and tried to smile. Mommi had better come. She'd promised he'd be home for Three Kings Day, and that wasn't going to happen. She could at least visit him tonight and bring a couple of presents.

Just after the show started, Stew and his dad sat down in front of him, near Pookie. They laughed and pointed as Dwane danced.

Benni didn't care what they did. He was too nervous to watch Dwane, anyway. He kept turning around and checking the door. *Where was Mommi?*

At intermission, Mrs. Pukowski stood up, smiled and said, "Come get some punch and cookies with us, Benni."

Benni shook his head and leaned over to Pookie. "Ask Mr. Bolton if my mother's coming, okay?"

Pookie frowned. "Ask him yourself. What if I say something stupid and make things worse?"

Benni scowled. "You won't. Just do it, okay?"

Pookie shrugged. "Okay."

Benni followed Pookie and his mother to the dining room. He didn't see Ronnie or Mr. Bolton anywhere.

"HEY, IT'S THE LATINO LOSER!" Stew yelled as he and his father hurried by. "WHERE'S YOUR MOTHER?"

Where's yours?

Benni kept walking and looked at the floor. The fist in his stomach was curling and uncurling. He'd like to show Stew who was boss again, but no way was he going to be in time-out when Mommi showed up.

"Maybe your mother got lost," Stew sneered over his shoulder.

That did it. Benni turned around and headed back to the gym. He didn't want cookies, anyway.

A few minutes later, he was chewing on his fingers as he watched people returning for the second half of the show. He wondered if

Mommi had missed the bus, or forgotten the date of the program. He wondered if she was sick or drunk.

Tears stung his eyes. Who was he kidding? Mommi wasn't coming, not even for Three Kings. His head began to pound, and the fist in his stomach squeezed on his supper, trying to get rid of it.

He had to get out of here.

Benni grabbed Pookie's arm. "I feel bad, Pook. Tell Ronnie I wanna go to the room, okay?"

In a minute, Ronnie was there, feeling Benni's forehead. "No fever, Benni. What's wrong?"

Benni looked at Pookie.

"It's like this," Pookie said. "Benni ate a whole lotta beans and enchiladas for supper, you know what I mean?"

Ronnie smiled. "Okay, ma man, let's go upstairs and get you in bed."

Benni felt exhausted by the time he reached his room. He dropped his jeans on the floor, climbed slowly up onto his bunk, and lay with his face toward the wall. He couldn't stop the tears and he didn't try. He let them wet the pillow. He didn't wipe his nose.

Go away Ronnie.

Ronnie stood near his head. "Wanna tell me what's wrong? You upset 'cause your mom didn't come?"

Benni pulled the covers over his head. *I don't talk, Muscles, especially about Mommi.*

Ronnie sighed. "Well, if you won't talk, I can't help you. I don't know why she didn't show. We sent the Parents' Night invitation to her new address, and it didn't come back. I'm sorry, buddy. Listen, I'll be down the hall in the TV room, sorting clothes, except when they're giving out awards. Call me if you need something, okay?"

Won't happen, Ronnie. I need Mommi, and she's not coming. Serves me right for turning her in.

A few minutes after Ronnie left, Benni threw the covers off. His blankets felt like lead. He'd tried to sleep, but the faces of Mommi and Poppi and his friends from the city ran through his head like a video. He wondered if anybody from home remembered him or even cared about him.

Probably not.

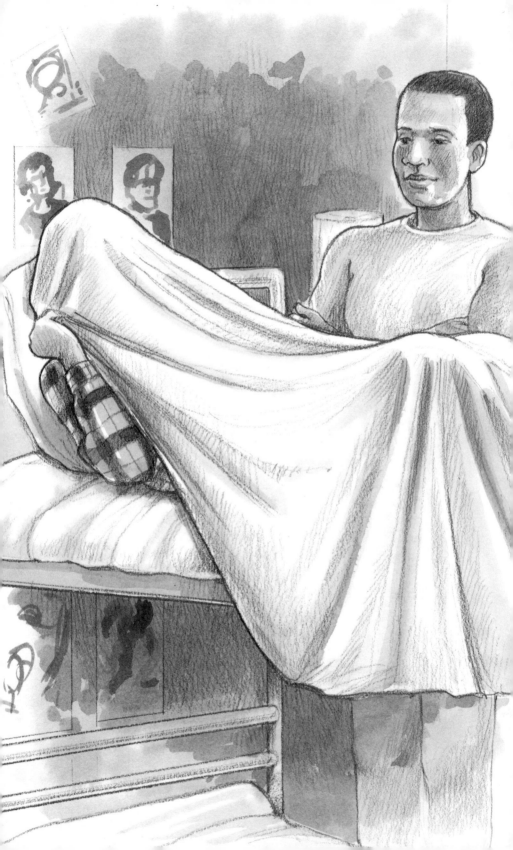

Victoria might. He remembered her squeaky little voice and how she'd asked him for help. He loved her bouncy red curls, and those eyes that looked like the sea. She'd understand how he felt.

Pookie didn't. Pookie kept saying that Mommi would come through, but *his* mom visited every weekend. Pookie didn't know what it was like to be let down, time after time.

Victoria did, though. She wouldn't care if he cried. She wouldn't laugh if Benni said he was afraid he'd never see Mommi again. She missed her family, too. She worried about them. He wanted to talk to her.

All of a sudden, he didn't feel tired any more. He sat up. There was still time to go to the chapel. He could be a good friend even if he wasn't a good son.

Quickly, he pulled on his jeans and jacket. Then he carefully bunched up his pillow and clothes under the covers until they looked like a sleeping body, in case Ronnie came back.

He stood for a moment and listened at the door. Hearing nothing, he crept out into the hall. Ronnie wasn't in the TV room, but Benni's heart pounded in his ears when he realized he might meet Ronnie on the stairs.

He made it to the first floor without being seen. The show was still on, its music blaring from the gym. Benni ran toward the kitchen and slipped out the back door.

Outside, it was dark and bitterly cold. Drifting clouds covered the moon and most of the stars. Icy snow crunched and collapsed under his feet, sending long cracks ahead of him as he crossed the meadow.

Inside the chapel, it was only slightly warmer, and so dark that he had to feel his way down to the cellar, then up to the foyer. Under the choir loft, he tripped and cried out in pain as his hand hit the hard plaster wall.

Barely breathing, he stood statue-still and listened. If Victoria had heard him yell like the first time, she'd return.

He waited for the warmth and smoky smell of Victoria's beautiful chapel, but it stayed dark and cold.

Reaching out in the dark for a stack of pews, he dumped one over and waited again.

Silence.

"VICTORIA, IT'S BENNI! WHERE ARE YOU?"

Mommi didn't visit tonight. I need to hear you sing. I want to talk to you.

Silence.

He kicked a pew, wondering why he'd thought Victoria would be different from anyone else. She didn't care about him. She'd probably forgotten him already. What was he doing here, anyway?

He must have imagined the whole thing. There never was a tiny girl or soft yellow light.

As he turned to leave, he bumped his knee on the pews he'd knocked over and remembered the pain in his foot the first day. He hadn't imagined that.

No, the chapel had been beautiful, and there was a Victoria.

He wasn't giving up. His eyes had grown used to the dark and he could see a little better. He hurried up the choir loft stairs. Maybe if he dumped the organ bench like Sarah had, Victoria would come back.

Once in the choir loft, he realized his mistake. There was no organ up there any more, and no bench. Just a few chairs and a heavy old table.

"How can I find Victoria if her furniture isn't even here?" he cried, running at the table. With his body, he bumped it across the room until it slammed against the wall, knocking a huge piece of plaster to the floor.

"OWWWWWW!" Benni yelled, shaking his sore wrists and rubbing his stomach.

Next time, stop running when the table hits the wall, stupid.

And then his heart skipped a beat as he heard Victoria crying and watched the soft glow of lantern light roll across the loft like melting butter.

Chapter 7

Victoria sat on the top stair, her head in her hands, her tiny shoulders shaking.

Benni's body was air again, but he didn't feel afraid. He was so glad to see her. "You heard me, Victoria!"

She stood up and wiped her eyes. "I heard an explosion and yelling. I thought it must be you. The girls will arrive soon for evening services. I left dinner early because I was not hungry."

Benni looked guiltily at the wall behind the organ. The plaster was perfect again and the table was gone. "You heard me smashing the wall with a table."

Victoria frowned. "You must not keep breaking things and knocking things down, Benni, or there will be no chapel for me to return to...Not that I want to be here. I want to see Edward and Mamma."

She bent in two again, sobbing. Her tiny back and lovely red curls were all that Benni could see.

He felt helpless. How could he help her find out about her brother when he couldn't even walk right?

He flew to a window near the loft, saddened by her tears. Outside, the meadow stretched darkly for a long distance. There were no street lights or cars on the road; no lights twinkling in nearby houses.

He turned quickly and flew back to her. At least he could listen. "What's wrong, Victoria?"

"Our cook, Tessie, saw Aunt Mary in town this morning. She said that Edward is so sick, Mamma cannot leave his side, even to write to me. I fear he will die and I shall never see him again."

Benni didn't know what to say. He didn't know how to comfort Victoria. When he worried about Mommi, no one could comfort him.

"Victoria, why can't your mother visit you for just an hour?"

Victoria shook her head. "She dares not leave Edward. Tessie said he cannot move one side of his body, or speak. He has trouble breathing and is very quiet." Tears ran down her cheeks. "Edward is never quiet. Mamma is also afraid to visit me for fear she might give me diphtheria, even if she herself is not sick."

"Hasn't the doctor given Edward a shot yet?" Benni asked.

Victoria frowned. "Why should the doctor shoot my dear little brother?"

Benni sighed. How could he explain a shot, when they probably weren't invented yet? "Never mind, the doctor will cure him."

Victoria stood up and stamped her tiny foot. "How can you say that, when so many children have died? The doctor can do nothing. NOTHING! He could not save my cousin or my friends." She leaned on the bannister and sighed, wiping her eyes.

Benni looked back at the windows. He was surprised at the brightness of the sky. "The clouds have gone away, Victoria. The stars and moon are shining now."

Victoria stepped back and straightened her shoulders. "Yes, it is a beautiful night, and I must stop crying. I cannot help Edward this way, and 'tis not enjoyable for you either, I am sure. Come with me. I will show you the barn."

"The barn?" Benni didn't move. "Will I go back to my own time if I leave the chapel?"

"Not if you're with me," Victoria said.

As they left the chapel through the front door, Benni stopped in surprise and stared across the meadow. The buildings of his Oak Grove School were gone. In their place stood a large, beautiful square mansion with a flat roof. Lanterns outside revealed that the building was painted in three shades of green with fancy wood trim at the roofline and on its porch railings.

Behind the house, he saw three smaller, shed-like buildings. Where the parking lot should have been, stood a huge, two-story barn.

"This is Oak Grove Seminary for Girls, my aunt's school," Victoria said proudly.

Benni followed Victoria toward the barn. "But where is my Oak Grove?"

Victoria thought for a minute. "The girl I met here once said that part of the Seminary house and all of the barn burned down long ago. They must have torn down what was left, and built your Oak Grove after that."

She walked quickly, pulling her heavy cape around her. "Come. You must see the lovely gelding that Aunt Mary bought last week," she said.

"What's a gelding?"

Victoria's head dropped and she looked at the ground. "Em...A gelding is a male horse that has been...changed." As if to avoid any more questions, she ran ahead of him to a large door in the center of the barn.

Benni looked down at the main road. The moon shone across grassy fields where he'd seen an old farm house that day. The main road was narrow, muddy, and deeply grooved.

He followed Victoria into the barn, ignoring the door and zipping through the wall. He found himself in a room full of carriages and equipment. The room was large and dimly lit by several oil lamps. Victoria stood smiling and talking to an old man who sat on a box, cleaning a saddle.

"Hello," Benni said to the man, who didn't reply. Benni jumped up and down and waved his arms. "This is fun," he said, zipping through the man.

Victoria scowled at Benni.

"Certainly you may visit Apollo, lassie," the man said.

"Thank you, Hector." Victoria lifted a lantern from a hook on the wall and hurried to a nearby stall.

"Benni," Victoria whispered, "No one but I can see you. You must not distract me like that." She patted the neck of a very large horse. "How do you like Apollo? He is very strong, and pulls our school carriages very fast, but we cannot use him now. We are forbidden to go to town, because of the diphtheria."

She whirled around. "But you are not forbidden to leave, Benni! You could go to my house and find out how Edward is."

"But will I still be in your time if you are not with me?"

Victoria frowned. "No, I think not."

"Besides, how can I find out how Edward is if your mother can't see or hear me?"

Victoria thought for a minute, then happily clapped her hands together. "I know! I could follow you to town secretly. Then I would wait outside my house while you enter Edward's room. You could tell me what you learn."

Benni shook his head. "No, you might get sick."

Victoria sighed. "Perhaps I would. Maybe you could go alone to my house and call me from there. Perhaps my house would change if I heard you singing my favorite hymn, 'Abide with Me.' I heard that girl from another time singing it, remember?"

"Teach it to me," Benni said, and listened carefully as Victoria sang:

"I fear no foe, with thee at hand to bless.

Ills have no weight and tears no bitterness.

Where is death's sting? Where grave thy victory?

I triumph still if thou abide with me."

Benni liked the tune, but wasn't sure what the words meant. "What does "if thou abide with me" mean?" he asked.

"It means," Victoria said softly, "that I will be all right if you will stay with me and help me."

Benni smiled. "I'll try to, Victoria." She seemed strong in so many ways, yet she needed and trusted him. She had become his special friend; he wasn't alone any more.

Listening carefully as she sang the verse, he joined in more each time she repeated it.

Suddenly, the chapel bell rang four times. Victoria stopped singing and listened. The bell rang again, four times.

"NO!" Victoria screamed. "FOUR KNELLS! Edward is four years old! Please, do not let it be Edward who is dead!"

Before Benni could react, Victoria had left the barn. He followed her outside. Moonlight bounced off her curls as she ran across the meadow to the Seminary house and fell, sobbing, into the arms of a tall woman who pulled her quickly inside.

The dark mansion wavered like grass under water and disappeared.

Instantly, Benni's Oak Grove was back, and he was standing in the parking lot. The moon still glowed, but there were bright lights everywhere.

He felt cold to his bones. Victoria was gone, and he still hadn't helped her.

Maybe there was nothing he could do, if Edward was dead. His stomach clenched. Maybe Victoria wouldn't need him any more.

Sadly, he snuck back inside, undressed, and lay on his bed, ignoring the music downstairs and humming Victoria's hymn.

"Abide with me, Victoria," he whispered, "And I will stay with you."

Chapter 8

A few days later, right after lunch, the intercom crackled as the school secretary distracted Benni's class during math. "Phone call for Benni in Mr. Bolton's office."

"Go ahead," Ms. Williams told him. "You can do the last page later."

Benni hesitated. *How can I take a phone call if I don't talk?*

Mr. Bolton handed Benni the phone when he walked in. "Jakob has something to tell you."

"Hey, Benni, how are you?"

Just great, Jakob.

"Your mother called me yesterday. She's doing better: no drugs or alcohol and living with some new people. She still doesn't have a job, though, which is why she didn't send you any presents for Three Kings Day."

And she couldn't let you know until now?

"Benni, are you there?"

No, I left.

Jakob sighed. "I wish you'd talk to me. Anyway, she thinks she can get a ride to Oak Grove next week. She'll call Mr. Bolton when she knows the day."

She's coming to see me?

"I hope you'll talk to her when she visits."

Don't worry, I'll talk to her. I'll talk to ANYONE if she visits me. He skipped and hopped like Dwane all the way back to class. Maybe she'd forgiven him after all.

By the time Benni returned to his classroom, Miguel, a chubby third grader, was standing in front of the class holding a small wooden box. "The night before Three Kings Day," he was saying, "a lot of Puerto Rican kids put hay or grass in a box for the camels that went to Bethlehem. I guess those camels were real hungry when they got to my house, 'cause they ate all the grass and left me this good stuff!"

He tipped the box forward. Inside were baseball cards, a watch, a small video game, bubble gum wrappers, action figures, and a pencil sharpener shaped like a car.

Benni felt the fist in his stomach tighten up. He used to get toys for Three Kings, too, before Poppi left and Mommi started drinking.

He picked up his pencil and glared at his open math workbook. He didn't feel like doing math. Instead, he turned the page and drew an ugly Mommi with ragged hair and crossed eyes. *She was stupid. She couldn't get a job or an apartment.*

His pencil moved to the next page. *Poppi was ugly and stupid, too.* And the next. *This school was...*

"What are you doing, Benni?" Ms. Williams asked, pointing at his workbook.

Oops. He'd ruined the next three pages in his workbook. He took a deep breath and the fist loosened up.

Ms. Williams flipped several pages in his book. "Benni, you know we're short on math books. I can't give you another one, and I won't be able to read your answers through these pictures. I'm surprised at you."

I'm surprised at me, too, Ms. Williams. I don't know why I did it.

"Can you tell me why you did this?" Ms. Williams asked.

"Tell her," Pookie whispered. "Say something."

Benni shook his head.

Pookie jumped out of his seat, waving his arm. "Ms. Williams, I know why Benni drew all over his book! It's those hyper arms! Sometimes, up in the room, he'll be all quiet. Then, all of a sudden, his muscles go BLAAAAAAAA and he writes on the first thing he sees. He can't help it, honest!"

Ms. Williams ignored Pookie. "Benni, if you're angry and you want to draw instead of talk, that's fine. But you know it's against the rules to destroy school property. You've just lost half your afternoon points."

Benni put his head down on the desk. *There goes my trip to town. Sorry, Victoria. I've let you down because of my stupid temper.*

He picked up his pencil and started erasing the pictures he'd drawn.

An hour later, Ms. Williams was smiling at him.

"Congratulations, Benni. You've earned your points back by doing extra work and following all the rules."

Benni punched his fist high into the air. *Yes!*

"Keep it up," Ms. Williams said, "And you'll make Honor Roll this term."

"Now you can go to the movies on Saturday," Pookie whispered, smiling broadly.

And maybe I can find Victoria's house, in case Edward didn't die.

After supper, Ronnie and Betsy, another dorm counselor, set up a volleyball tournament in the gym. Once Benni's team was out of the game, he slipped down behind the bleachers and snuck out the exit door.

Running to the chapel, he was so excited, he barely noticed the cold. Finally, he had good news for Victoria. He had enough points to go to town, to her house, on Saturday!

"VICTORIA," he yelled as he entered the dim sanctuary of the chapel. "IT'S ME, BENNI! HEY, I'M HERE!"

He ran up the choir loft stairs and looked around. The table he'd shoved against the wall was still there. In the moonlight, he could just make out thin strips of wood behind the hole he'd made in the plaster. It looked terrible.

Victoria was right. He shouldn't destroy the place to find her. He sat down on the top stair and began to sing "Abide with Me." A minute later, he stopped, confused. What was the fifth line? He started again, stopped again, punched the floor. What a dope! They'd sung that verse together so many times. He should know it by now.

At least he knew the tune. He hummed the hymn loudly, but she didn't appear. He sang "LA, LA LA LA" to the tune, almost shouting it.

Still no Victoria.

He descended the loft stairs slowly, leaning on the bannister. It would have been so great to see her pretty little face light up when she found out he was finally going to town.

Fear, like ice cold water, suddenly crossed his stomach. Maybe, he thought, she wasn't listening for him because she didn't need him any more. Maybe he'd never see her again.

He jumped to the floor from three steps up. "WHO CARES!" he yelled and shoved a pile of pews so hard, they fell with a bouncing BA-LAM! BAM BAM! BAM!

Immediately, smoothly, the old chapel faded like a scene in a movie, its dusty darkness replaced with soft lamplight, the smell of burning wood, and a gleaming, simple beauty.

A handsome older woman stood at the pulpit, reading from the bible by candlelight. Benni looked around the room and saw Victoria staring solemnly at him from a pew nearby. She sat between a stern-looking woman and three older girls.

He smiled. How sweet she looked with a small white hat perched on her red curls. Her dark blue velvet dress was trimmed with white ribbon and a soft, lacy collar. He wondered why she wore a plain, black cloth band around her upper arm. It didn't go with her clothes.

Suddenly, Victoria started coughing loudly. The woman next to her scowled, then whispered something into Victoria's ear. Still coughing, Victoria hurried from the sanctuary and Benni zipped after her into the foyer.

"Nice work," he said.

"What is it, Benni?" Victoria asked. "I thought I heard you trying to sing my hymn just now, but I dared not search for you in the middle of services. Then I heard the crash."

"I didn't break anything," he assured her, "I just wanted to tell you that soon, I'll be going to town. I've been thinking about you and Edward. The last time I saw you, you were afraid that the bells..."

And then he realized why she was wearing a black band. It must be a sign of mourning.

Tears slipped onto Victoria's cheeks. "The bells did toll for Edward. He is dead and Mamma is so exhausted from taking care of him that I still cannot see her."

"I guess you don't need me to go to town, then," Benni said, picking nervously at his fingers.

This is it. Thanks, but no thanks.

Victoria wiped her tears, looked back at the chapel doors and coughed again, loudly. "But I do need you, Benni. I am so glad you finally can help me. You must go to my house at five-eight-six Main Street and call me from there. Then we shall find out if Mamma is ill, too."

Benni sighed deeply. Victoria still needed him. "I'll try," he promised. "Keep listening for your song."

Victoria smiled, nodded and stepped outside the chapel. Benni shivered as a deep cold and dusty darkness instantly slid around him.

He ran back to the school and hurried inside. At least he hadn't been gone very long. He'd sneak back to the gym and find out who was winning.

"THERE you are!" Pookie said from the landing as Benni ran past the main staircase. "Get upstairs, QUICK! We've been lookin' all over for you. Stew and Whip started fightin', so the game broke up early."

Benni took the stairs two at a time. "Say I was hiding under the bleachers."

"We checked there before we left."

"Say I was in the lav."

"Ronnie looked there, too."

Benni stopped on the third floor landing and thought. "Say I was in the kitchen looking for food."

Pookie's light eyebrows shot up and he gave Benni the "thumbs up" sign. "Hey, great lie! You're improving, Ramirez."

Benni grinned. "Had a good teacher."

As they rushed through the doors to third floor, Benni took one look at Ronnie and knew he'd never believe Pook. Ronnie was standing in the hall, supervising the kids in the john. He looked like he could tear phone books in half, easy.

"Forget lying," Benni whispered to Pook. "He's in no mood."

Ronnie stormed over to Benni. "Where ya been, Ramirez, pickin' mushrooms?"

Benni shrugged and walked to his room without a word. Ronnie followed him, scolding loudly while Benni got ready for bed. "You are in big trouble," Ronnie said, leaning against their lockers with his bulging arms folded against his chest. "Didn't you realize how worried we'd be if you took off, Ben? We looked all over for you. Betsy even went outside. Don't you know that AWOL—away without leave—is against the rules and means AUTOMATIC loss of a week's privilege points?"

Ronnie was still spouting as Benni crawled into bed and pulled the covers over his head.

Good thing I didn't tell you exactly when I'd be in town, Victoria. Looks like it'll be a while.

Chapter 9

The next morning, Benni woke up to a Reveille tape being played loudly in the hall outside.

"Betsy's on today!" Pookie said. As usual, he jumped out of bed instantly, while Benni scrunched down under the covers, hoping Pook wouldn't whomp him before he left for the lav.

A few minutes later, Pookie returned. "FINE, GET IN TROUBLE!" he yelled in Benni's ear, "BUT I'M GONNA BE ON TIME FOR BREAKFAST. FIRST BELL ALREADY RANG!"

That woke Benni up. Only fifteen minutes left to shower and dress. He ran into the empty john and rubbed a dab of toothpaste over his front teeth. Then he stood under the shower just long enough to get wet and wrapped a towel around his waist. He'd comb his hair and...

"Oh, no! You are not clothed, Benni!"

Victoria! What was she doing here? He looked at her filmy body and shivered. "Now you're the ghost, Victoria."

"Of course," she replied. "Just as I was on the day you came to Oak Grove."

Benni's mouth dropped. "You were the smoke in the closet?"

"Yes, and the shadow on your window," Victoria said. She looked at the floor, her cheeks turning a delicate pink. "But I must go. It is wicked for me to be here when you are..." She covered her eyes.

"Wait," he pleaded, "I have something important to tell you. I'll get dressed." Hopping and puffing, he pulled on his underwear, jeans, and shirt, then threw his towel into a basket near the door.

"Okay, look! I'm decent now."

Victoria peeked through her hands. "Oh, thank goodness." She pointed to one of the showers. "Is that what Papa called a rainbath when he wrote to us about his hotel?"

"Maybe," Benni said. "We call them showers."

Benni opened a stall door. "Check this out."

She flew to the toilet, where she stood, ankle-deep, in the water. "What is this?"

"It's a toilet." He stopped, afraid he'd embarrass her and she'd leave. "It's like...an outhouse."

"Outhouse? Oh, you mean, a back house, where you..."

Benni nodded and turned toward the mirror, combing his hair quickly. "How'd you find me, Victoria?"

She flew back to him, balancing delicately on the edge of a sink. "I can find you in this part of the building anytime. It is over the Seminary cellar."

"But I wasn't singing just now."

"No, but I went looking for you, so you didn't have to sing."

"Oh." He put down his comb. "Why were you looking for me, Victoria?"

Tears rolled down her cheeks. "Tessie came to see me last night. Mamma is in bed now, she is so exhausted. Aunt Mary is in New York, and my father's passage home will take weeks. I am so lonely, and so worried about my mother. Please help me visit her."

"But if I go to your house in town and call you, the house will change to your time, and you'll be a real girl, right? You might catch diphtheria if you go there."

Suddenly he felt afraid. *I might catch diphtheria.*

"I won't go near Mamma," Victoria promised. "I will just stand outside her window and talk to her."

"Then why don't you go to town yourself?"

"I have tried to when I am a specter, but I cannot leave the Seminary buildings. Perhaps if you call me from town, I could. Please, Benni, help me. I have not seen Mamma for three weeks."

"BIG DEAL!" Benni yelled, then blinked away tears. "I haven't seen my mother in nine months."

Victoria's hand flew to her mouth. "Oh, Benni. I am so sorry. I did not realize it had been so long since you saw her. Is she ill?"

He sighed. "You could say that. I'm sorry I yelled at you. Come on, let's practice your song so I can find you easier next time." For all he knew, her house might be torn down by now, but he didn't want to worry her.

Victoria's eyes shone bluer than ever through her tears. "You shall help me go to town, then?"

"Sing," he said.

He ignored the second bell. Helping Victoria was more important than breakfast. He'd say he was sick so he wouldn't lose points for missing a meal.

When he was sure he knew all the words, Victoria gave him directions to her house, then faded away, smiling. He continued to sing her song, concentrating so hard that he didn't hear the guys come back from breakfast to get their books.

Then Stew stuck his head in the lav.

"Hey, STARSTRUCK, whatcha doin', tryin' out for the opera?"

During supper that night, Ronnie left the table to talk to Mr. Bolton. Stew watched him go, then elbowed Tang, a little Asian kid, in the ribs. Tang was small and skinny and stuttered badly.

Uh, oh, here he goes, Benni thought, as Stew grabbed Tang's roll and held it high. Stew always bullied the little kids.

"G-give it b-b-b-back," stuttered Tang.

"Put it back, pus bag," Benni said, giving Stew a menacing look.

Stew licked the roll, grinning.

Benni grabbed Stew's roll and gave it to Tang. "Here, lick it," he said.

Tang licked the roll, smiled at Benni, and took a long drink of milk.

Stew leaned into Tang's face. "Atta boy. Drink lots of milk so you'll pee your pants at supper. That's the only place you haven't done it so far, BABY."

Tang hung his head. Everyone knew he wet the bed sometimes and once he wet his pants in school. They just didn't rub it in.

Stew looked around to make sure Ronnie's back was still turned. Then he grabbed Tang's hair, pulled his head back, and tried to pour the rest of the milk on Tang's mouth, which was clamped shut.

"BETSY, LOOK AT STEW!" Pookie yelled.

Stew let go of Tang fast.

Betsy frowned. "I didn't see what you were doing, Stew, but I'm sure it wasn't good. One more complaint, and no TV for you tonight."

As soon as Betsy turned back to her own table, Stew gave Tang an Indian burn. "Don't get me in trouble again, Chink, understand?" Then he looked at Pookie. "And here's what snitches get," he sneered, pouring the rest of his milk on Pookie's plate.

Pookie jumped up and shoved Stew.

"HEY, BETSY!" Stew yelled. "POOK PUSHED ME!"

Pookie sat down. "Great. Now I'm in trouble," he said.

Betsy stormed over to their table. "All right, what's wrong with you guys? Are you trying to get in trouble, or what?" She looked at Pookie. "No TV tonight for you, Mr. Pukowski, for shoving."

The fist in Benni's stomach was ready to go. Stew started the whole thing and Pookie was the one who got punished. It was time to teach Stew a lesson. He leaned over and ground his heel into the top of Stew's foot.

"OW, CUT IT OUT!"

"Is there a problem, fish mouth?" Benni asked.

Stew leaned back and tried to pull his foot away while Benni pushed down even harder.

Betsy turned around. "NOW what's going on?"

Benni lifted his foot and Stew fell off the bench.

"OWWWWWWW," Stew yelled and grabbed his sneaker.

Betsy ran over. "What's the matter, Stew?"

"Benni stomped me and I didn't do nothin!"

Betsy took off Stew's sneaker and sock and moved his foot around in a circle. He yelled like she was cutting toes off.

Then Ronnie hurried back to the table and looked at Stew's foot. "Okay, okay! Calm down, Stew. Your foot's a little red, but I don't think it's broken. Dwane, get me some ice from the kitchen, okay?"

Dwane ran off and Ronnie looked at Benni. "Wanna tell me what happened here?"

Benni shrugged his shoulders.

Ronnie scowled. "Okay, Pookie, what happened?"

Benni held himself around the middle so he wouldn't laugh. Pook would think of something.

"Gee, I don't know, Ron. We were just sittin' here, eatin' supper *nice as pie,* and all of a sudden, Stew starts screamin'. Hey, he tripped on the way in. I bet that's when he hurt his foot. He's just tryin' to get Benni in trouble."

Benni smiled at Pook. *Thank you, good buddy.*

Ronnie sat down and looked around the table. "Anyone else have an explanation here?"

Nobody said a word.

"All right," Ronnie said. "Let's forget about it, okay?" He uncovered the three casseroles on the table. One was filled with soggy green beans, one with noodles, and the third oozed with a thin, brownish gravy full of white lumps of meat.

Benni turned his plate over. It was bad enough he had to live at this stupid school. He wasn't eating their disgusting mystery meat.

"What's the matter?" Ronnie asked. "Aren't you hungry, Ben?"

Not any more.

"It's the tapeworm babies," Pookie blurted out.

Benni looked up. *This should be good.*

Ronnie raised an eyebrow, but Pookie didn't take the hint.

"Really, Ron. Every couple weeks, the tapeworm in Benni's gut hatches her babies. They chew on him awful, and it hurts so bad he can't eat."

Ronnie sighed. "Thanks for the insight, Mr. Pukowski. Listen, Ben, if you don't like the meat casserole, just eat some beans or noodles."

I'll eat when I don't get sick looking at the food.

Ronnie stared at him for a minute. "Are you sick, Ben?

I was fine until you served garbage. Benni shoved his plate away, knocking over his milk.

"Watch your temper," Ronnie said. He grabbed some napkins and handed them to Benni. "We don't force kids to eat food they don't like, but you have to eat something because it's a long time 'til breakfast." He lifted one eyebrow. "Or you can lose your points for the night. Up to you."

The fist in Benni's stomach was hard as rock. What good were privilege points, anyway? Staff just took them away, first chance they got.

"I need thy presence, every passing hour..."

Benni sat up straighter and listened. What was that? It sounded like Victoria, like her hymn.

"I triumph still if thou abide with me."

He'd forgotten about her and his promise to help her.

He took a deep breath and the fist opened up.

He wiped up the rest of his milk and righted his plate. Looking away from the glop in the meat casserole, he spooned some noodles and beans onto his plate, kept his eyes down, and ate every last morsel.

For Victoria.

Chapter 10

The next morning, Pookie's hair flopped up and down as he jumped around, frantically pulling on his jeans. "I can't believe you're ahead of me. I always get up first," he puffed.

Benni tightened his belt. "Ha! Beat you!"

"Kiss mine, Mr. Quick. So what's goin' on?" Pookie asked. "There's gotta be a reason you woke up before me, and I know it's not breakfast."

Benni sat on the chair. "Shut the door."

"A-ha!"

"Listen, Pook. I need a favor. This'll sound strange, but trust me, okay?"

Pookie snorted. "Why not? You're ALWAYS strange."

"Cut it out, Pook. This is important, but I can't tell you why."

I could die if I don't find out, that's all.

Pookie's eyes got big. "Are you in trouble?"

"No, but I need some information from the nurse, and I can't ask her myself."

"Why not?"

"'Cause I don't talk to adults, remember?"

"Oh, right, so what do you want me to do?"

"Say you're sick after breakfast and go to the nurse. Then, when no one's around, ask her if kids die of diphtheria. If she says yes, find out how they get it, okay?"

"What's dif-ther-i-a?"

"A disease."

Pookie shrugged his shoulders. "Okay, no big deal."

Downstairs, Benni watched Pookie suck in a mountain of scrambled eggs, three sausages, four pieces of toast with jam and butter, two glasses of milk, and a handful of Chocolate Krispies.

Anybody would believe you're sick, Pook, ANYBODY.

Including Ms. Williams. She didn't know Pookie could eat Brazil and not even burp. So when Pookie said, "I don't feel so hot, Ms. Williams. Somethin' I ate, I think," Ms. Williams looked very concerned. "A stomachache, Pookie? That's too bad. Here's the Health Room pass."

Benni hid his smile behind his science book.

You should be in the movies, Pook.

An hour later, Pookie strolled into art, the picture of health. He sat down next to Benni and started drawing. "Okay, here's the story," he whispered out of the side of his mouth. "Just one problem: I had to tell the nurse who wanted to know about diphtheria. She *made* me."

Benni's shoulders slumped. *Mr. Bolton better not hear about this.* "Weird Benni wants to know about strange diseases, Jakob."

Pookie brushed his hair out of his eyes. "The nurse said kids don't get diphtheria any more. A long time ago they did, and most kids under twelve died of it. Sometimes, even an adult died of it. But, you know all those shots you get when you're a baby? She said we've had all those shots. That's why we don't catch it any more."

Benni smiled. *I'm safe! I've had all my shots. I can help Victoria and not get sick!* "Thanks, Gold Medal Liar."

Pook didn't even look up. "No problem, Ramirez. I'll take candy *or* money."

Chapter 11

Several days later, in social studies, Benni sat hunched over his desk, wishing he were somewhere else. All the other fifth graders had given their oral reports and Ms. Williams was sitting a few desks behind him, tapping her foot.

"I said, you're next, Benni," she repeated.

Benni had worked hard on his water pollution project, but he wasn't doing an oral report. No way.

"I'm waiting," Ms. Williams said, louder. She stood up.

Benni looked at Pookie.

Pookie raised his hand. "Ms. Williams, Benni did all the work, right?"

Ms. Williams nodded. "He did all the written work, but one-third of this grade is for the oral report. Benni has to give one like everybody else, or he loses thirty-three points."

"Better do it," Pookie said under his breath.

Benni stared at his desk. *I don't talk to adults about anything.*

Ms. Williams stood up. "Are you refusing to do your oral report, Benni?"

I'm refusing to talk until Mommi comes and gets me.

Pookie jumped up, waving his report. "SEE THIS, Ms. Williams? Benni helped me so much with my report last night that the talk part of his brain got all frizzled up. It don't work any more."

Benni looked at his desk so he wouldn't smile. *It's true. I'm brain damaged.*

Ms. Williams rolled her eyes. "Sit down, Pookie. Benni, if you don't do your oral report, your grade falls to a D. That means you'll have to stay after school today and do extra credit work."

Benni shrugged. Ms. Williams closed her grading book with a bang and walked to the reading table at the back of the room. "Okay, I want the Bitter Ice group over here."

Benni took a deep breath and sighed loudly. He hated oral reading. He always got a check and lost points for not reading out loud. Tang read after Benni refused to, slowly and carefully because of his stuttering.

When Tang finished, Stew, who sat across the table from Tang, leaned into his small, tense face. "Do you have a p-p-problem, sa-sweet cakes?"

Jaleesha, the new girl in fifth grade, gave Stew the evil eye. She was tall and wiry, her skin a soft, medium brown. Benni liked her looks, especially her long, fuzzy hair, but she had proven on her first day at Oak Grove that she had extra-tough city ways. No one teased her any more.

Stew sat back and stared at his book.

"Good thinking, boy," Jaleesha muttered.

Ms. Williams put a behavior check on the paper in front of her. "That's two checks, Stewart, for teasing. One more check, you're in time-out, and you lose twenty points."

She handed Tang a paper. "Tang, I want you to look up your vocabulary words. Benni, will you please take him to the other table and help him?"

Stew made the "brown nose" sign at Benni behind Ms. Williams' back. Benni ignored him.

At the work table, Benni opened the dictionary. "Okay, Tang, do you know how to do this?"

Tang shook his head. "I n-not go to school at ho-home."

Benni picked the easiest word in the list, 'apple'. "Say apple." Tang did. "Now find the first letter of apple in the dictionary."

Tang found "a," then "ap," then "appl." "Th-there it is!" he said with a big smile. "Ap-ple! I f-found it!"

Benni smiled back. In a few minutes, Tang could find the words by himself.

"Hey, you're a pretty smart kid," Benni said.

"Hey, you're a pa-pretty sa-smart teacher."

Ms. Williams smiled when she saw Tang's paper. "Looks like you two are a good team. Thanks for helping Tang, Benni. You did a great job. I think I'll give you fifty extra points, for being such a good teaching assistant."

Yes! Thanks, teacher. Now I have enough points to go to town on Saturday and look for Victoria's house. I won't lose them this time.

"MS. WILLIAMS!" the intercom boomed. "Please send Benni to the office right away."

Benni's face fell. He ran toward the main hall, his stomach in a knot. He'd tried to do everything right today. He'd made his bed and turned in his homework. He even went to breakfast. What was wrong?

Maybe he wasn't going to town after all.

Chapter 12

When **Benni reached the office,** he found Mr. Bolton talking on the phone and Victoria floating over his desk, hopping from one foot to the other.

She flew to Benni anxiously. "Thank goodness! I have looked everywhere for you!"

"The school wing and the gym are not over the Seminary foundation," he murmured under his breath.

"Oh, I see." She whizzed to the door, then back through Mr. Bolton to the window. Benni stared at the sky blinking blue through her curls. *Why was Victoria so hyper today?*

"How come you were looking for me?" he asked, not moving his mouth.

Mr. Bolton put his hand over the phone. "Benni, your mother's on the line. Want to talk to her?"

Victoria flew to the desk and pointed to the telephone. "You can talk to your mother on this?"

Benni ignored her and shook his head "no" to Mr. Bolton, who was holding the phone out to him.

I'll talk to her when she shows up, and that's it.

Victoria flew to his side. "Benni, I searched for you because I am frightened. Tessie has not sent a message to me in a week. Maybe she is sick, too, like Mamma."

Mr. Bolton scowled in Benni's direction. "I'm afraid Benni doesn't want to talk, Mrs. Ramirez. He hasn't been speaking to adults lately. If you tell me what you want him to know, I'll repeat it."

Victoria started hopping again. "Are you going to town soon, Benni?"

Mr. Bolton nodded. "Okay, I'll tell him, Mrs. Ramirez." He moved the phone away from his mouth. "Benni, your mother says that her boyfriend's promised to bring her to Oak Grove on his next day off. They want to take you out to lunch. How does that sound?"

The fist in Benni's stomach squeezed hard.

It sounds about as good as the last promise she made, Raysie. She doesn't care about me any more. Why should she? She's got a boyfriend with a car and some money. He's with her all the time and I haven't seen her since last spring. I'm supposed to sit around and talk to HIM, the first time she comes here?

"No way!" he mouthed, his head down.

Victoria put her hands on her hips. "You are so foolish, Benni. You said your mother was poor. Does she have her own carriage? Maybe she must accept her friend's help. At least she is coming to see you. At least you can talk to her."

She wiped her eyes. "I cannot see my mother, or talk to her on that—that talking machine. I think you are a most stubborn and ungrateful son."

Benni felt the fist in his stomach explode. What did Victoria know about him, or Mommi? What right did she have to say he was ungrateful? He jumped up and dove at her. He almost shouted, too, but saw Mr. Bolton's amazed look just in time.

"Um, listen, Mrs. Ramirez, why don't you call me when you know what day you're coming? I think Benni will talk to you then. He's doing all right at Oak Grove. I'm sure he'd love to see you."

Victoria shook her finger at Benni. "You say you miss your mother, yet you will not talk to her. I do not understand you."

Mr. Bolton hung up the phone. "Benni, I'll let you know when your mother's coming to visit," he said. "I hope you'll talk with her when she arrives."

Benni stood up. *Yes, sir! No problem. Mommi's still in Nowhere Land with a boyfriend instead of me. What good are you, anyway?*

He ran out of the room before he yelled or kicked something, he was so mad.

Victoria floated down the hall at his side. "Why were you so rude to your mother?"

"Look, *Stupido*, I'm not talking to my mother until she shows up here, get it? I want to SEE her, not talk to her on the phone. I want to LIVE with her, not visit her. GET IT?"

Victoria looked shocked. "I think you are cruel and selfish, Benni."

He walked faster. *Who cares what you think?*

Victoria floated behind him, pale, silent, and sad.

"Just go away, Miss Ghost. Who called for you, anyway?"

"But, Benni, I thought you wanted to talk to your mother."

Benni's voice echoed in the empty hall. "You thought I wanted to talk to her, because you thought I was like you. You thought my mother was like your mother. You thought my father was like your father. Well, you thought WRONG. You don't know anything about me or my life."

He turned around and spat his words like darts. "You've got it so easy, Victoria. You have a mother and a father and an aunt. They love you and take care of you. You live in a big house. You have servants."

He slapped the wall. "Well, here's the deal, Miss Perfect. I'm NOBODY and I've got NOTHING. Now GO AWAY!"

Her tiny, cloud-like body disappeared long before he reached his classroom, but all day, he remembered her sad little face and the pearl-like tears that hung on her cheeks.

His head pulsed with a steady throb that mimicked her sobs and a pain that hurt him every bit as much as he'd hurt her.

Chapter 13

At recess, Stew waited until Tito, the sixth grade aide, left to take a fourth grader to the nurse. Then, after he made sure Ms. Williams wasn't watching, Stew grabbed Pookie's basketball, the one his mother had given him for Christmas.

"GIVE IT BACK, STEWBALL! You can't have it. It's mine!"

"DO IT," Dwane screeched, "OR I'LL GET YOU. MY BROTHER'LL GET YOU, HEAR?"

Stew tripped Dwane. "I'm so scared, big boy!" he sneered. Dwane sat rocking on the ground, holding his leg. "GET OUTTA HERE!"

Benni grabbed Tang's arm. "Go get Ms. Williams, okay?"

Stew held the ball high over Pookie's head, his ugly green eyes squinting with pleasure. "Ooooo, baby butterfingers wants his ball!" He whirled around, kicked Dwane again, and knocked Tang down.

Uh, oh.

Benni had seen Stew in action before. Pretty soon, he'd really start beating on the little kids. He looked around. Ms. Williams was way over at the gym door and Tito hadn't come back yet. That took care of getting help.

When Pookie grabbed for his ball again, Benni jumped on Stew's back and pulled his hair so hard that his head fell back. Stew dropped to his knees.

73

"Give me the ball, slimeface," Benni warned, pushing Stew's head toward the ground. Stew groaned and twisted, but Benni held on. "I said give it back or you'll be BALD."

Stew's face turned red as he tried to stand. "MAKE me, lice head."

Jaleesha ran over, her fists clenched. "That's right, Benito, hurt him! When you done, it be MY turn. I'll fix him GOOOD."

"Don't do it, Jaleesha," Benni said. "You'll lose your points. Just hold him down when I get off. You, too, Pook, so I can get Ms. Williams."

He gave one last killer yank on Stew's hair, and Stew dropped the ball.

"NOW!" Benni yelled. Jaleesha and Pookie held Stew down as Benni slipped off his back. Benni jumped up, grabbed Tang's hand and helped Dwane up. "LET'S GO!" he yelled.

Dwane and Tang laughed all the way back to the gym.

"You sh-showed him," Tang said.

"Yeah, you were GREAT!" Dwane yelled. "You just like the Rayzor Broth-ahs in my neighbahood. They let you in, sure."

Right. I'm a hee-ro. That's why I live here.

After lights out, Pookie was still talking about recess. "You took care of Stewball, all right. You can be on my team any day."

"Thanks a heap, Pook."

Pookie pushed up on Benni's bunk with his feet. "Hey, I didn't say you were perfect, Ramirez. I just said it was great you helped me and the little kids. It's not so great you won't talk to staff. I'm sick of lying for you. I guess you're still my best friend, anyway."

"Thanks, Pook. I don't want you to get hit by a truck, either." He felt lucky to have a friend like Pook. Pookie was good at forgiving.

Benni wished Mommi would forgive him. She must still be mad that he turned her in. She didn't show up for Three Kings Day, she called Jakob more than she called him, and she never wrote.

Maybe Victoria was right. Maybe he should have talked to Mommi when she called. He should have said he was sorry and told her he was doing okay in school. He should have told her he helped the little kids.

Drying his eyes, Benni turned his pillow over.

Too late now.

Chapter 14

The next day, after Benni finished his math problems, he decided to draw his father. He hadn't seen Poppi since he was six. He hoped he could remember what he looked like.

First, Poppi's hair. Dark and curly with a piece in front that fell over his forehead.

Dark brown eyes, but they didn't look right. Benni had drawn them round, but he remembered them better as narrow when Poppi was mad.

He wanted to forget about that, so he drew Poppi in a good mood, like when he and Mommi were getting along. He sighed. There was no way to draw what he liked most about Poppi—his husky voice and his big, fast laugh when he felt good.

The mouth was right: chin up and just a little smile. The nose was okay, too. Long and straight, never broken. Big shoulders. Strong hands holding a hard hat and a hammer.

Where was Poppi, Benni wondered. Was he still working in construction?

He probably had a new family now, and a new son. Benni's stomach tightened painfully. *He probably loves his new son more than me.*

He wouldn't know me if he bumped into me on the street. He hasn't seen me in almost five years. He doesn't love me, and I sure don't love him.

Benni ripped up the picture and pushed the pieces into a pile, like a deck of uneven cards.

I guess I'm like the other losers here. Oak Grove was full of kids whose parents weren't around. Dwane's father was gone, too, and his mother didn't want him. Pookie's father was dead and Stewball's mother took off when he was a baby.

He wished he could talk to Victoria about this, but she wouldn't understand. She had a nice mother and a rich father who took good care of his family. She was too sweet, too innocent. She was from another world.

How he missed her.

Suddenly, his stomach clenched in fear. *Maybe Victoria hates me, I was so mean to her the other day. Maybe I've scared her away forever.* He didn't want to believe he'd lost her. He liked her and wanted to be with her again. She made him feel important because she needed him. She made him forget his problems.

He decided he wouldn't make the same mistake with her that he'd made with Mommi, if Victoria came back. He'd tell her he was sorry. He'd tell her he was wrong.

Benni jumped as Tang grabbed his arm.

"My fa-father want you go to d-d-dinner with us to-to-to-night. I tell him o-k-kay?"

Benni looked at Poppi's ripped-up picture. He knew it wouldn't be like going out with Poppi, but it might be fun.

"Sure, I'll go, but tell him I don't talk, okay?"

Tang's father was small and thin and not much bigger than Benni. "Thank you for helping my son," he said seriously, shaking Benni's hand. Then he took them out for pizza and let them order anything they wanted.

Benni devoured his pizza and drank two giant sodas while he watched Tang's father carefully pick the pepperoni off his pizza. Tang's father seemed very nice. He listened carefully to his son and didn't make fun of his stuttering or get mad when Tang spilled his soda. Benni could see that he was a good father. So, why didn't Tang live with him?

"Ask your father to tell me why you're at Oak Grove," Benni whispered to Tang.

Tang's father looked sad when he heard the question and tears brightened his eyes. "My wife come to U.S. first," he said softly, "She die right after she come, hit by car. I not know where she is, where Tang is. I find out at Embassy in New York. Now I have job. When I have apartment, I take Tang home."

He patted Tang's arm. "That be soon, I promise."

Tang's head dropped. His shiny black hair covered his forehead, but Benni could see tears on his lashes.

"Oh, I almost forget! Look what I bring you!" Tang's father pulled out two small cars and a puzzle book. "Two gifts for you, son, and one for Benni."

Tang gave Benni the book. "You are g-good at w-w-words," he said with a shy little smile.

After Tang's father dropped them off at Oak Grove, Tang went straight up to his dorm. Benni watched him go, then squeezed into the closet under the stairs. He didn't feel like being with the guys. They'd be getting ready for bed: laughing, yelling, chasing around. He needed to be alone for a while, to think.

Tonight, watching Tang and his father, he'd remembered how Poppi used to hold him when he got hurt and hug him when he went to bed; how Poppi carried him on his shoulders at parades and play-fought when they watched wrestling on TV.

He didn't put all that in his picture of Poppi. He didn't show how much he loved Poppi and how much he missed him. Benni put his head on his knees and cried. He had friends here, but no family.

When he lifted his head, Victoria was there, glowing gently in front of him.

"Hello, Benni," she said softly.

"Victoria, I'm sorry I yelled at you the other day. I was wrong to yell at you. I was mad at my mother for not visiting me or taking me home, not you."

"I understand, Benni. You did hurt my feelings, 'tis true, but I upset you very much, and I am sorry."

Benni wiped his eyes. "Is that why you're here?"

"No," she said sadly. "I was lonely. Aunt Mary is back from New York but she is nursing three girls who are very sick, and teaching, as well. She has no time for me."

"I thought your father was coming home soon."

Victoria nodded. "He is, in two weeks, but Mamma is too sick to visit or write to me." Her sob hung between them. "It is so hard to wait, alone, for Father, and for news of Mamma."

He nodded sadly. "I know how you feel, and I think I can finally help you."

"Help me? How?" Victoria jumped up excitedly, her head and shoulders disappearing through the ceiling of the closet, then dropping down again.

"Saturday, I'm going to town," Benni explained. "If your house is still there, I'll call you with your hymn. Maybe your house will change to your time when you find me, like the chapel does. If you don't go near anyone, I think you won't get sick."

"And Mamma will be there, and I can talk to her, or peek in her window!" Victoria wiped her cheeks. "Oh, thank you, dear friend."

"LIGHTS OUT, GUYS, TWO MINUTES!"

Benni peeked into the hall. "That's Ronnie. If I don't go upstairs right now, I'm DEAD."

"Thank you, Benni. You kept your promise. You are a real, true, friend."

Tears stung his eyes. No, she was the real friend, like Pookie. She forgave him.

He watched her fade away, then ran up the long, wide staircase past second, to third floor. Ronnie was so busy yelling at Whip he didn't see Benni slip into his room.

Pookie was already in bed. "You're crazy, ya know that, Ramirez? You're *this close* to big trouble, every day."

Benni yanked off his jeans and threw them at the chair. "I know, but it sure is great, living on the edge."

"Right. Now get into bed, cliffhanger, 'cause Ronnie's on his way."

Benni hopped up the ladder and dove under the covers.

Seconds later, Ronnie looked in. "Both here? Great. Good night."

After Ronnie left, Benni let out a long, low whistle. *That was close, too close.*

"Ronnie was here ten minutes ago," Pookie whispered, "Lookin' for you. I told him you didn't make the lav in time and were down in the laundry room, washing out your shorts."

Oh, thanks, Pook.

Chapter 15

On Saturday afternoon, Benni sat near the back window of Oak Grove's big blue van as he rode to town with Ronnie, Tito, and eight other kids who'd made their points that week. In a few miles, the wide country fields had disappeared, and houses started to crowd closer together. Stores of all kinds whizzed by, and when they reached town, he saw lots of cars and even a bus.

It's not Portland, but it'll do.

"Hey, keep it down back there!" Ronnie demanded as they drove into the parking lot behind the old theater.

Benni, Pookie, and the other kids yelled, "SURE" and then made even more noise.

Benni smiled. He'd finally made enough points to go to town. Everyone was in such a good mood, they wouldn't notice if he snuck out for a little while. He'd find Victoria's house, call her so she could talk to her mother, then run right back to the theater. Simple.

"You finally made it, huh, Benni?" Tito said with a smile.

Benni smiled back. *Finally.*

A few minutes later, he and Pookie sat in the theater's next to last row of seats, inhaling popcorn and watching coming attractions.

"You'd better make your points next week, too," Pookie said, pointing at the screen. "See that movie? You don't want to miss it. My cousin said it's the best."

As soon as the feature started, Benni handed his popcorn bucket to Pookie. *This is it.* "I need a favor, Pook."

Pookie scrunched down in the seat. "I have a feeling I'm not gonna like this."

Probably not. "I want you to cover for me, Pook. Anyone comes looking for me, I'm in the lav, okay?"

Pookie's wide, friendly face turned serious. "Where are you goin', Ben, really?"

"I can't tell you, Pook, but I'll get back as fast as I can. I've got to do something important."

Pookie frowned, then shrugged. "Okay, just be fast. Don't forget, you've already been AWOL once."

Outside, it was bright, more like early spring than winter. Benni looked up and down Main Street.

"My house will be easy to find," Victoria had said. "It's at the top of the hill next to the church and is big and square, with a large carriage house behind it."

Benni found it easily. It was a two-family house now, with mail boxes near the front door and a paved parking area in back. The paint was peeling and some of the trim was broken, but he could tell it was beautiful once.

He ran up the driveway to the back door and pulled on the knob. "It's unlocked!" he gasped. He couldn't believe his luck. Still, he felt strange, walking into someone else's house. He wiped his hands on his pants and took a couple deep breaths. He wouldn't be doing this if he didn't care so much about Victoria.

Just inside the door, stairs led up to a landing and then turned right. Beyond the stairs was a short hall with two doors opposite each other.

He opened the left door. Stairs down to the cellar. The door on the right had a sign that said "Apt. A." He decided to go upstairs first. The upstairs door read, "Apt. B."

He pressed his ear to the door.

No music, no dog barking, no baby crying. He knocked loudly.
What would he say if someone answered?

Excuse me, is Gordie home? Yeah, that would do it.

He knocked again. No answer.

One down, one to go.

He banged on the door downstairs and waited. Banged again
and waited again. Nobody home.

Yes! Here goes, Victoria.

In the hall, he loudly sang the first verse of Victoria's hymn, the
one about someone staying with you when you were alone and out
of luck. It was about him and Victoria, in a way.

He waited a minute, then sang again when she didn't appear. He
must be too far from Oak Grove. Or maybe he had to be inside one
of the apartments to call her. He tried the door to Apartment A.
Locked. He ran upstairs. Same thing. Tried the cellar door. *Not locked!*

He walked down old wooden stairs to an unfinished cellar. It was
dusty and full of junk.

His stomach was churning. This was taking too long. What would
he do if someone came home? He'd better get out of there, quick.

"You are a real, true, friend."

He jumped. Victoria had heard him, she'd come! He whipped
around. No, she wasn't here, and the room hadn't changed.

He must have imagined her voice, but at least it had reminded
him of his promise. He sang her favorite verse twice more, but she
still didn't appear.

He rocked from foot to foot, wondering where she was. He was
trespassing, walking around in someone's house. He could be arrested! Not only that, if Ronnie found out he'd left the movies without permission, he was dead!

Calm down, Ramirez. He took three deep breaths.

Okay, one last try. He banged on some boxes and shouted her
song, but no luck.

Sorry, Victoria. Sadly, he crept up to the first floor and listened at
the hallway door. Quiet. He slipped out the rear door and ran all
the way back to the theater.

Pookie was pacing in the lobby. "You're in TROUBLE, Ramirez.

Tito's in the van with the other kids and Ronnie's talking to the manager. I'm supposed to be watching for you."

Benni smiled. "Well, I'm back. Did you tell Ronnie I was in the lav?"

Pookie shook his head. "He was so mad when he found out you were gone, I forgot to lie. Where were you?"

"Pickin' mushrooms, okay?"

Pookie looked hurt.

"I'm sorry, Pook. I had to do something, I can't say what."

And you wouldn't believe me if I told you, anyway.

They headed for the manager's office.

"Pook, tell Ronnie I was throwing up from too much butter on the popcorn."

Pookie's eyebrows went up. "Not bad. Your lying skill is approaching the Mastah's."

Benni snorted. "HA! Nobody can lie like you."

But Ronnie didn't buy it, even from the Mastah.

"Throwing up, MY FOOT, Pukowski! I checked the lav first thing, remember? He wasn't in there."

Oops. Olympic Lying Team just struck out.

Chapter 16

Jakob opened the door of a room next to Mr. Bolton's office. "We can talk in here, Benni."

The room was small and crowded with furniture.

Benni walked to the window, his back to Jakob. Jakob sat down on one of the overstuffed chairs. "I hear you're still not talking."

Benni looked out the window. *You hear right.*

"But I also hear you're doing well in school and you've made some friends. In fact, Ms. Williams said you're very good to the younger boys. So, I think it's time we found a family for you."

Benni spun around. *What?*

Jakob held up his hand. "Don't get nervous. It'll take a while. It's just that your mother isn't doing her job."

Job? Mommi doesn't have a job.

"You see," Jakob continued, as if he'd read Benni's mind, "It's your mother's job to go into a drug rehabilitation place, kick her habits, and get her life together. She can't get you back until she's drug free and has a place to live."

Benni was confused. *What does that have to do with me going to a new family? Oak Grove isn't home, but it's all right. I don't want to go somewhere else.*

"Anyway," Jakob added, "I'm not sure she'll ever be able to take care of you, and you deserve a good home. You belong in a family."

Yeah, my family.

He wished he could go back to Puerto Rico and live with his aunt or his grandmother, but Jakob said they had too many problems.

"I know you want to live with your mother," Jakob said. "But she's not doing any better now than she was a year ago, so we're going to court soon..."

Court! Was Mommi arrested again? Benni's hand flew out and knocked over a lamp.

Jakob picked it up. "You look scared, Benni. Tell me what you're afraid of."

Benni felt like a stone was pressing on his heart.

What do you think I'm afraid of? You're taking Mommi to court!

Jakob sat down again. "You probably think I'm the bad guy, trying to take your mother's rights to you away, but I want you to belong to somebody, maybe even get adopted. I want you to grow up in a family where someone cares about you more than they care about drugs and alcohol."

The stone on Benni's heart shattered and the pieces hurt. Jakob was right. Benni remembered what it was like when Mommi's bottle was empty or she didn't have any dope. That was when she didn't worry about whether he had lunch money or if there was toothpaste in the bathroom. She didn't care if his shirt was clean or if his shoes fit.

But she was his mother. Even if she didn't get better, he didn't want new parents. He didn't want new parents!

Benni ran for the door. *Jakob can take Mommi to court, but he can't make me stay here and listen.*

"Benni, wait, please."

Benni stood at the door, his forehead pressed against the wood.

Where am I going, anyway, upstairs so scummy Stew can laugh at me?

Jakob's hands were strong on Benni's shoulders, like Poppi's. His voice was soft. It rolled over him, easing the ripples in his stomach.

"I'm sorry I have to do this, Benni. I hope it will help your mom choose a different life. She'll get the court notice this week. If she goes into a drug treatment program before the court date, then you two may have a chance to be a family again. I don't know any other way to tell her she's in deep trouble."

She's not in deep trouble. I am. She's throwing me away.

"Do you want me to try to call her now? Will you talk to her?"

Benni shook his head. *Why should I? She doesn't care about me.*

"Okay. Then let's hope she makes the right choice, Benni. It's you or drugs."

Benni felt like he couldn't breathe. *That's it? THAT'S THE CHOICE?*

He pulled away and ran up to his room, stumbling, falling on one knee, blinded by tears.

Me or drugs, me or drugs. He kicked his door shut and flopped on his bunk.

Choose me, Mommi, not drugs. ME. He felt hope slip away with his tears.

But why should she? She hadn't chosen him for years. He lay still as a stone.

Maybe he'd lost her forever.

Chapter 17

On Monday, right after school, Benni trudged up the long, wide stairs to Oak Grove's attic behind Ronnie.

"Now don't get nervous," Ronnie warned, "I know the attic's big and crowded." He hit the light switch and Benni stared.

Big? The attic was HUGE and it was crammed with mountains of stuff.

"You know," Ronnie said, "If you'd told me why you left the theater Saturday, you might not even be here. This not-talking thing gets you in a lot of trouble."

Talking about Victoria would get me in more trouble.

Benni leaned on a post and folded his arms on his chest. *No way can I clean out this place. Five custodians couldn't clean out this place.*

"Look, I know it's big," Ronnie said. "But you can do it. Other kids have done it. This job will always be here, because people keep giving us junk, and junk usually ends up here."

Then let them clean it out.

Ronnie waved his hand. "Hey, we're not talkin' the whole attic, you know, just the main part here."

Oh, that's good.

"So, here's what you do, every day this week. First of all, you'll

have to finish your homework during recess. After school, you eat your snack, then come straight up here and work. Betsy or I will check on how you're doin' before supper."

What if I'm doing nothing?

Ronnie scratched his chin. "Of course, last year, we had a kid who got a week of attic cleaning, too, but he decided to sleep instead of working. He had to go to bed after supper three nights in a row for that, and then work three extra days for foolin' around." Ronnie raised his eyebrows. "Any questions?"

Yeah. What genius thought this up?

"Then I guess you understand," Ronnie said. "Here's some leaf bags for magazines and trash." He pointed to several uneven stacks of cartons in the middle of the room. "See those boxes? Check each one out. If they have books or junk in them, put 'em near the stairs. But if you find any old records, put them under the window over there. Mr. Bolton will want to look at them."

Why does he want old records? Nobody plays them any more.

Ronnie looked around. "By Friday, I bet you'll have this place lookin' good and ready to sweep, ma man."

Can't wait, ma dorm counselor.

Benni grabbed a trash bag as Ronnie left. He'd work fast and rest later, since he was missing his free time before supper, too. He quickly filled three bags with old magazines and junk, but the boxes in the middle of the room were beginning to get to him. What was in them, anyhow?

He lifted a box from the tallest stack, opened it up, and sneezed. Moldy old books. He put the box by the stairs.

The next box was full of chipped baseball trophies. He put it near the first one. The third box held yellowed files marked with kids' names and "Date of Entry" on the front. He opened a file marked "Amelia Jones, Date of Entry: April 6, 1931." Inside were her birth certificate, school reports, health records, a record of her father's visits, all kinds of records.

Records! These were the records Ronnie was talking about.

Benni looked at the door. *I shouldn't be reading this stuff. What if Ronnie comes back early?*

Oh, well. He picked up the next record, marked "Thomas Tilson, Date of Entry: December 29, 1929." The writing inside said that

Thomas's mother died in childbirth and his father killed himself a month later when the stock market "crashed."

Benni sighed. *At least my parents aren't dead.*

He pulled up the rest of the files and checked the date of the last one at the bottom of the box. The dates of entry were getting older. The last one was 1924.

He sat back on his heels. Maybe there were even older records in the other boxes! He dropped that box next to the window, ran back and opened several more. Each box with files contained about three years' worth of records. Some were from recent times, like 1968 or 1974, but some were from the early 1900s.

Excitement whizzed inside him. How old did these records get? Maybe he'd find some from Victoria's time!

Benni's arms and back soon ached from carrying the heavy cartons over to the window, but he ignored the pain and worked even faster when he heard the free time bell ring. Finally, he found records from 1899.

YES! He jumped up and danced around. *1899! 1858 wasn't much earlier!* There must be records from Victoria's time right there in the attic! They might say when her mother got sick and when she got better!

Benni knew he had to tell Victoria about this, but wasn't sure he had enough time to call her before the supper bell. He decided to take the chance. She'd be so happy to hear of his find, and he wanted to see her happy for a change. For once, he wanted to see her lively, sparkling blue eyes shine with joy instead of tears.

He sang softly, sure that she'd hear him, because he was over the old school.

But she didn't. He sang louder, until he was almost shouting, watching the door the whole time for Ronnie.

Hurry up, Victoria.

Finally, she appeared, but she looked exhausted. Her beautiful blue eyes were faint and half-closed. Her filmy body seemed smaller than ever and flickered weakly, like a candle in a draft.

"Victoria, what's wrong?"

"I'm a-weary," she said in a raspy voice. "And thirsty. My throat hurts."

"Then I'm sorry I called you," Benni said, his own throat tightening up. He felt scared. She'd always looked so strong, so full of energy. What was wrong with her?

"Do not be sorry," she assured him softly. "I wanted to know when you were going to town."

Benni swallowed. "But I went already—last Saturday. I found your house and sang and sang, but you didn't come. Maybe you can't leave Oak Grove!"

Barely visible tears slipped from her eyes. "Perhaps not, because I did not hear you. You were in my house, and I did not hear you." She sobbed weakly. "How will I see Mamma if I cannot even go home?"

He shrugged. "I don't know. I'm sorry it didn't work out, but at least I have good news for you." He patted the box next to him. "This box has student records that go back to 1899!"

Victoria gasped and straightened up a little. "Records from 1899? Oh, Benni, you are wonderful. Perhaps my record is in one of these boxes. When will you know?"

"I'll go through the rest of the boxes tomorrow after school, and then I'll call you, if you're not too sick. Do you have a cold? I can wait until you're better."

Victoria shook her head. "No, do not wait. Call me. I must know. Aunt Mary has sent for Doctor Ellsworth, although she does not think I have diphtheria."

Diphtheria! The word hit him like a punch in the stomach. *The nurse had said diphtheria used to kill children, before they had shots for it.* Benni's heart began to pound furiously.

Maybe Victoria has diphtheria, and that's why she's so sick. Oh no, don't let her die of that.

The bell for dinner rang through him like a shock.

"Victoria, leave right now!" His voice trembled like his body, but she didn't seem to notice. "Ronnie'll be here any minute."

She flickered away weakly and he dropped to the floor, his head on his hands. He wished he'd never met her. He was tired of loving people and having them leave him.

"No," he said, sitting up. "I'm not sorry I met Victoria. I'm just sorry I have to say good-bye."

Chapter 18

All the next day, Benni thought about Victoria. He remembered her tired eyes and worried about her husky voice.

He wondered if she was dying. He was afraid she'd never be free if she didn't find out what happened to her mother.

It was so hard to feel responsible for her. He wasn't special. He'd never done anything special in his whole life and Victoria was asking him to do the impossible.

In art class, he found himself drawing her sweet little face. Her eyes were filled with love, and he knew he loved her back. He had to help her find out about her mother, even if it meant she would disappear forever.

As soon as Ronnie left him in the attic that afternoon, Benni grabbed a leaf bag and filled it in no time. Then he checked every box left in the pile. When he'd looked through all of them, he wanted to scream. None held student records older than 1899.

He sank to his knees. *Now what?*

He'd looked at everything in the attic. Unless...Benni sat up. Maybe the oldest records were stored somewhere else at Oak Grove! He'd look around downstairs tonight.

But Victoria had seemed so sick the last time he saw her. Tonight might be too late. Where could he look now?

The cellar! He ran downstairs, ducking into closets or lavs when anyone approached. Finally, he made it to the kitchen and down the back stairs.

The cellar was damp and musty, but not as crowded as the attic. Benni worked quickly, opening boxes and cabinets, checking behind every door. Finally, he found a large closet under the old school built of stone and lined with cedar. It smelled earthy.

He pulled on a string near his head and squinted at the sudden, bright light. Three file cabinets lined one wall of the closet; dusty floor-to-ceiling shelves filled another.

His stomach tensed as he pulled out the top drawer of the first file cabinet. Inside were old books and crumbling medical records. This might be what he needed! He felt hopeful and happy. Without thinking, he sang Victoria's hymn.

"Benni, I...barely...heard you."

He spun around. Victoria stood trembling in front of him, paler and weaker than before. Worst of all, she breathed very fast, almost gulping air.

Blinking away tears, he shut the drawer. "How are you, Victoria?"

"I fare quite poorly," she said hoarsely, "But eight of the Seminary students fare worse. They have diphtheria and are in the chapel, which Aunt Mary has turned into an infirmary."

Benni's body froze. The disease was spreading through the school. Victoria must have it, too. He swallowed hard so he could talk. "The records upstairs stopped at 1899, but yours might be here."

She grew fainter. "Oh, I hope so. I must lie down, I am so tired. Benni, will you get sick, talking to me? I do not want to make you sick."

Her eyes fluttered and she started to fall. He stepped forward to hold her up, remembering at the last minute that she was a cloud.

"Victoria, listen," he said loudly. She straightened up again. "Don't worry about me. I won't get sick. Babies get special medicine now so they don't catch most serious diseases. I got that medicine when I was a baby."

He fought to hide his tears. If only she'd gotten that medicine.

"Go back and rest," he said. "I'll call you as soon as I find out anything. Remember, listen for me all the time."

Victoria's body wavered; her eyes closed again. "I will try to listen, Benni. I will try to stay awake. I must know about Mamma, I must."

As soon as Victoria left, Benni raced to the file cabinets and started searching again. He found no records older than 1880.

As he closed the last drawer, he heard Ronnie calling him. He crept upstairs, dashed into the nearest bathroom, and flushed two toilets.

Please, Ronnie, believe this is where I've been and this is what I've been doing.

Chapter 19

Supper stuck in Benni's throat and hurt his stomach, but he forced himself to eat. He knew he might be up all night, looking for Victoria's record.

When dessert came, his head dropped. No way could he play basketball after supper and pretend everything was okay when Victoria might already be dead.

Ronnie put his hand on Benni's forehead. "What's wrong, Benni?"

"He don't feel good," Pookie said.

And that's no lie.

"I believe it," Ronnie said. "No basketball game for you tonight, ma man. Come on, I'll help you get to bed."

Benni felt much better by the time he and Ronnie reached third floor, although he didn't let Ronnie know it. Now he could start searching for Victoria's record right after Ronnie left, instead of having to wait for lights out.

In the john, Benni moved slowly and acted like he had lead weights on his legs and arms. Ronnie put Benni's clothes in the hamper, then helped him up to the top bunk.

"Betsy's down the hall," Ronnie said as he gave Benni a damp towel to put over his eyes. "I'll ask her to look in on you later."

Before Benni left for the cellar, he lay in bed, searching the old closet in his mind. He didn't want to miss a thing. He'd checked all the file cabinet drawers. Now he had to look in the boxes and books on the bottom shelves. Last were the big, old-fashioned notebooks that Victoria called ledgers on the top shelf. He'd go through everything.

When Benni heard the basketball game start in the gym, he tiptoed past third floor's TV room. Betsy was folding laundry, her back to the door. Carefully, Benni walked downstairs, trying to avoid the steps that creaked.

Once he reached the first floor, Benni breathed easier. No one was around; faint yells and thuds came from the gym. He'd have to work fast, in case the game ended early.

He ran downstairs and straight to the closet. Quickly but carefully, he looked in or at every single thing on the lower shelves. He found nothing from Victoria's time.

He began to feel more and more nervous. Maybe he was wasting his time down there and should be looking in the offices upstairs.

Sighing, he stepped onto a small stool and pulled down a short stack of ledgers from the highest shelf. He wasn't quitting yet. He had counted six stacks of the old books, each wrapped in heavy, clear plastic. He'd check them all.

The first three ledgers were in poor condition and dated in the early 1900s. Disappointed, he returned them to the top shelf and pulled down the next stack. This time, he checked only the dates on the last few pages of each book. Those books, too, went back on the shelf. Nothing before 1870.

Soon, there were only six ledgers left. He took down three more, trying not to cry. He knew he'd given it his best shot, but he still couldn't tell his little friend what she wanted to know most: what happened to her mother.

He blinked away tears. *Maybe it's already too late to help Victoria.*

Without much hope, he opened the next ledger, and gasped. This book was much older than the other ones! Its pages were browner and more fragile, its ink more faded. Carefully, he turned it over and looked at the date on the last page. It read, "31st May, 1859."

He sat on the stool and placed the book on his trembling knees.

Carefully, he lifted its cover. The first page read, "Journal of Mary Tyler, Founder of Oak Grove Female Seminary; in the Year of Our Lord, 1859."

Since it was now only a couple weeks after New Year's in his time and Victoria's, Benni read the entries for January, 1859. On New Year's Day, Mrs. Tyler began to write about diphtheria coming to Oak Grove. Entry after entry recorded the deaths of her students or their loved ones.

And then he saw it. "Today, my beloved niece, Victoria Regina Morgan, aged Nine Years, Two Months, followed her mother, my dear sister Anna, by two days, and her darling brother, Edward, by three weeks, to the grave. All felled by Diphtheria, O Horrid Disease!"

Chapter 20

Sobbing, Benni replaced the ledgers, stumbled up to the first floor, and ran outside.

Now he knew what had happened. Victoria had died of diphtheria, and her mother had died of diphtheria two days before she did. That's why she didn't know what happened to her mother. She was too sick.

I have to tell her, so she'll be at peace.

He wiped his eyes. He didn't want to tell her. If he did, she'd leave forever.

Inside, the chapel was cold and bare. He wanted to see it beautiful again, but he knew it wouldn't be. It would be a place to die, a place for Victoria to die.

He ran up the choir loft stairs, trying to swallow his sobs. He had to call her, or sing.

Loudly, he shouted her name, sang their hymn, knocked over chairs. "VICTORIA, LISTEN! HEAR ME! VICTORIA, WAKE UP!"

Unsteadily, the chapel wavered into life again. Its lovely drapes were closed. The chandelier and lights on the altar shone dimly. The stale air smelled of lamp oil and burning wood.

Gentle voices mixed with moans and rattling coughs as women dressed in dark gowns attended to the young girls who lay on narrow cots.

Benni's eyes rushed over the room until he saw Victoria lying on a cot in one corner. A tall, slender woman was wiping Victoria's brow with one hand and brushing away her own tears with the other.

He cried out, but no one heard him, including Victoria. She lay as still as a doll decorating a bed, her tiny body almost flat, her red hair spread over the pillow. She was perfectly still and perfectly beautiful.

He flew to her side. "Victoria, wake up!" he said loudly, but she didn't even stir. Her eyes were closed and she panted as if running a race.

"YOU BROUGHT ME HERE," he shouted. "VICTORIA! LISTEN AGAIN. LISTEN FOR ME! VICTORIA, IT'S BENNI!"

Trembling, he waited for a sign that she'd had heard him. Her coarse, desperate breathing, her skin turning blue, terrified him.

He sang her hymn loudly and shouted her name, but she only breathed more raggedly and turned more deeply blue.

He flew away, flew back, afraid that she would die before she knew what happened to her mother.

What could he do? He was a cloud. He couldn't shake her shoulders or squeeze her hand to wake her up. All he had was her song, her beautiful song.

He sang it again, shouting close to her head, over and over. Finally, her eyes opened and focused hazily above him.

"Benni," she gasped, "...Mamma?"

He leaned down, his mouth at her ear, and shouted. "YOUR MOTHER DIED TWO DAYS AGO, OF DIPHTHERIA! SHE'S GONE!"

Shock widened her eyes and then a tiny smile lit her face. She closed her eyes. "Thank you...dear...friend."

Suddenly, her back arched. A last, wavering breath escaped her body and she collapsed into a pose so peaceful that it looked like she'd never struggled to live.

Through his tears, Benni saw a womanly cloud of white reach

down and pull Victoria, now as filmy as he, from her body on the cot.

Immediately, the sickness, death, and flickering glow of the old chapel left with her, and he fell, sobbing and alone, to the cold, dusty floor.

When finally he ran outside, Victoria's hymn, all that he had left of her, rippled like water through his head. The meadow glimmered with moonlight and above him, stars winked unevenly. He turned his face upward and searched the skies.

"Good-bye, Victoria," he whispered, "Forever."

Already, he wanted her back, but he was proud that he'd helped her when she was scared and tired and sick. He stood straighter. *I'm not bad or stupid. I'm good. I'm strong, too. Strong enough to make it without Victoria; without Mommi, if I have to.*

He'd helped Victoria, and he'd helped Tang and Dwane.

Maybe now he could help himself.

Chapter 21

J ust as the class was lining up, Benni was called to come to the main office.

"Mr. Bolton's out," his secretary said, "But you can take your call in his office."

It was Jakob. "Hi, Benni. I wanted to tell you this in person, but I had an emergency."

Benni remembered Victoria and the dim, sad chapel. *That's okay, Jakob. I had my own emergency here.*

Pain stabbed through him again. He wished he could tell Jakob how much he missed Victoria and how he'd helped her.

"Your mother went into a drug rehab program last week," Jakob said. "At the hospital."

Benni sucked in his breath. *She's trying! Maybe she still loves me.*

"I know that's good news, Benni, but remember, she may not be able to stay straight when she gets out. We won't know for a while."

I don't care. I just want to see her. I know I can't live with her right now.

"Meanwhile, she's still your parent. The judge is giving her one more chance."

Benni's breath came out in a rush. *Our last chance, Mommi.*

He hoped she'd do better now. He hoped she'd visit him when she got out. He still missed her.

"But that leaves you at Oak Grove, Benni," Jakob went on, "For a long time, and you don't belong there."

Benni sighed loudly. *I've heard this song before.*

Jakob laughed. "You may not be talking, Benni, but I hear you loud and clear. I know it's hard to think about leaving Oak Grove, but I met some new foster parents last week. Their son just went into the Army and they miss having a boy around. Their little girl wants another big brother, too."

Good for her.

"I bet you'd like these people. I know this is sudden, but think about it, okay? I'll come see you next week."

Benni hung up and walked slowly to the dining room. He wasn't ready for this; he didn't know what to feel. He thought Jakob knew he didn't want to live with strangers again, or leave Oak Grove.

I just want my own family back, Jakob. GET IT?

Benni ate lunch slowly, ignoring the noise and confusion around him. He wondered how long it would be before Mommi could take him home. He wondered if she'd ever take him home. The thought of moving again after just a few weeks bothered him for the rest of the day, and even after lights out.

If Mommi never takes me home, then what?

Unable to sleep, he leaned over the bunk railing. "You awake, Pook?"

"Sorta," Pookie said.

"Jakob called me today. He wants me to go to a foster home."

"Yeah? What about your mother?"

Benni lay back on his pillow. "I can't count on her."

"You can count on me and Dwane," Pookie said sleepily. "We're your friends."

Benni sighed. "I know, but you're supposed to go home this summer, and Dwane said he's going to be adopted."

Pookie yawned. "Oh, yeah. Guess you can't count on us for long. Do you wanna live in a family?"

"Sure, my OWN, not a new one. These people might kick me out like the other ones, and I like it here all right. I like Ronnie and Betsy and Tito and Ms. Williams…"

"Yeah, but they're not around all the time like parents," Pookie said. "You never know who'll be on duty after school, or when you go to bed. It's not really like a family. I think you oughta try the foster home. It'll be good."

"I don't know. I'm sick of getting used to a place and knowing what to do, then BOOM, time to move. I'm sick of moving."

No answer except a snore.

Benni lay back on his pillow. *If only I could talk to Victoria. She'd understand why I'm afraid to leave. She wouldn't say it'll be all right, like Pookie always does, or punch me in the arm and run, like Dwane.*

He remembered how Victoria had yelled at him when he wouldn't talk to Mommi on the phone, when he wouldn't give her a chance. Maybe Victoria would yell at him now if he didn't give the foster family a chance.

In his mind, he heard Victoria singing her favorite verse, the one about someone who stayed with you, no matter what happened.

No one had ever stayed with him through "clouds and sunshine," through "every passing hour" like it said in the song, although Jakob and Pookie had stood up for him and watched out for him a lot.

He'd helped Victoria, and now she was gone. He'd watched over Dwane and Tang, but soon they'd be leaving. He couldn't count on people staying around for ever. It was time for him to watch out for himself.

The fist in his stomach softened. His life hadn't been that great so far, but it would be better someday if he worked at it.

Maybe he should give this foster home a chance. There was no guarantee it would work out.

And there was no guarantee it wouldn't.

Chapter 22

Right after school, three weeks later, Benni and Dwane watched as Pookie sat on the old suitcase that Jakob had dropped off the week before.

"Don't even try to open this thing 'til you get to the foster home." Pookie warned, snapping the latches shut.

"You sure you like these people?" Dwane asked, his voice softer than usual. "You only visited them three times."

Benni shrugged. "They're okay."

Benni leaned on his locker and wrote his new address on two pieces of paper. "If you guys write to me, I'll write to you."

"I'LL WRITE TO YOU!" Dwane yelled, grabbing one piece.

Pookie took the other piece, opened his locker, and put it inside his notebook. "I'm gonna miss lying for you," he said sadly.

The three boys jumped when someone knocked on the door.

Jakob looked in. "Ready to go?"

Benni nodded. Pookie kind of hugged him and Dwane yelled "BYE!" and ran out of the room.

As Jakob's car turned onto the main road, Benni loosened his seat belt, turned around, and stared at Oak Grove until it disappeared behind a curve. *Good-bye, Oak Grove.*

Good-bye, Victoria.

An hour later, Benni watched the street signs as Jakob drove off the highway and into a small town. Near the center, Jakob turned onto a wide street with small, well-kept houses on each side. Benni watched for number 59.

Soon, Jakob had parked in front of the small yellow Cape Cod house and taken the suitcase out of the trunk.

As he walked up the sidewalk to his new home, Benni remembered the garage in back and the basketball hoop next to the driveway. He also remembered what the house looked like inside, but it didn't feel like home yet.

Suddenly, he felt the fist tighten inside his stomach.

He was stupid, telling Jakob he'd move. He was crazy to leave Oak Grove, when he liked so many people there, when he felt safe there. Maybe he could still change his mind. If he left now, the foster mother wouldn't care. He wouldn't care.

He dropped his suitcase and looked back at the car.

Jakob's hand lightly touched his shoulder. "You didn't want to live at Oak Grove either, remember? I told you it was a good place, and that was the truth, right?"

Benni nodded. *It was a good place.*

"Well, this is a good place, too."

But still no Mommi on moving day.

"Your mother might visit you here some time. She's still in drug rehab and she's trying."

Benni looked at the pretty middle-aged woman who waited for them at the front door. She looked the same as he remembered: short, curly brown hair and eyes that crinkled when she smiled.

He picked up his suitcase again and tried to smile back.

"Hello, Mrs. Campos," Jakob said.

"Hello, Jakob and Benni." She stepped aside so they could walk in. "Let's put your things upstairs in your room, Benni, okay? Julio has taken my little Mira to the dentist, but they'll be home soon."

Benni led Mrs. Campos and Jakob to his new room. It was small, but he didn't have to share it with anyone. He put his suitcase on a chair and his treasure box on the dresser. *I'll find a good place to hide it later.*

Mira and her father were just returning as Jakob, Mrs. Campos, and Benni walked downstairs. Mr. Campos looked thinner in a suit, and taller, Benni thought, but his smile was just as wide as before.

"Hey," Mr. Campos said to Benni. "How about shooting some baskets before supper?"

Benni smiled and nodded.

Mira watched her father leave to change his clothes, hiding her face shyly in Mrs. Campos' dress. Benni thought Mira was cute, although she seemed small for a second grader. He didn't think she'd steal from him or call Mommi names. Maybe he'd read to her once in a while, or help her with her homework.

Shyly, Mira looked up at Benni, still hiding behind her mother. "I had a bad cavity, but I didn't cry, Benni. My dolly helped me be brave. She sang to me."

Proudly, she held up her doll for Benni to see. "Isn't she beautiful? She's my best friend in the whole world, and her name is Victoria."

Through his tears, Benni stared at the doll, so tattered and so loved. Her soft red curls were pulled back with a large, fluffy bow and her eyes were as blue as the sea.

Something warm curled inside him and made him smile. Someone was watching over him and loved him still.

Maybe he could talk to these people a little.

Maybe he would be all right.

Patricia H. Aust is a part-time school social worker who loves to write for children. She was "bitten by the writing bug" in fifth grade, when she rushed through her schoolwork to write poetry, stories, and plays. Since then, she has published several articles in social work journals, newspapers, and quarterlies. *Benni & Victoria* is her first children's book.

Mrs. Aust lives in rural Connecticut with her husband, where they enjoy visits from their son, daughter-in-law, daughter, future son-in-law, and the family's elderly dog, all of whom now live elsewhere.

Robert Sprouse is a free-lance illustrator who specializes in figure and portrait illustrations. He is on the faculty of the Alexandria, Virginia, campus of Northern Virginia Community College, where he teaches illustration and graphics. Mr. Sprouse lives in Arlington, Virginia. *Benni & Victoria* is his first children's book.